~~~~~~~~~~~~~~~~~~~~~~~~~~~~~~~~~~

ALMOST HUMAN

~ The First Series ~

Venomous Revelations

(Fatal Infatuation - Part 3)

by

Melanie Nowak

~~~~~~~~~~~~~~~~~~~~~~~~~~~~~~~~~~

Praise for Melanie Nowak's Venomous Vampire series

ALMOST HUMAN

"An emotional rollercoaster that has you sitting in suspense one moment, laughing out loud the next, and then crying your eyes out at yet other times. ALMOST HUMAN is definitely a book series that should be read slowly and savored."

- NightOwlReviews.blog

Winner of 2 *Literary Titan Book Awards* 2024,
Top 20 Author 2023 Amy's Bookshelf, Top Pick Night Owl Reviews
Best Vampire Series 1st place Winner by Public Reader Vote in
The Paranormal Romance Guild 2012 & 2015 Reviewer's Choice Awards

"I am officially making ALMOST HUMAN my must-read vampire series! The story is excellent. I am seriously impressed that the level remains consistently outstanding with each book. If you aren't reading this series, you should be!"

- NerdGirlOfficial.com

"ALMOST HUMAN departs from the common vampire tropes most delightfully with mesmerizing storytelling. Nowak's use of imagery stands out, painting a world that is haunting yet beautiful and rich with sensory detail. She also excels in her portrayal of character dynamics. Each conversation peels back layers of desire, curiosity, and doubt, with carefully chosen words that keep the reader guessing, intensifying the suspense, and deepening the intrigue. These exchanges are written with precision, emphasizing the power dynamics with a seductive pull most compelling. A highly recommended and worthy addition to any paranormal romance collection."

- Literary Titan Reviews

"Nowak wraps readers into her story, to live it with the characters. I love her attention to detail, development, and discovery. I didn't think the ALMOST HUMAN series could get even better, but it has!"

- ParanormalRomance.org

If you enjoy this book, please take a moment to leave a review online on your favorite book review website! Questions and comments can be directed to: WoodWitchDame@aol.com

You can get fun facts about this series and updates on book releases on the author's website at:
www.MelanieNowak.com

Original story Copyright 2004, Novella Copyright 2016
Melanie Nowak, WoodWitchDame Publications
Cover Artwork, Book formatting/Editing: Melanie Nowak
Cover Photo/Model: Natalie Paquette
http://natalie-paquette.wix.com/photos
http://fetishfaerie-photos.deviantart.com/gallery

VENOMOUS REVELATIONS
ISBN: 1944303030
ISBN-13: 978-1-944303-03-7

~~~~~~~~~~~~~~~~~~~~~~~~~~~~~~~

A Special Thanks to

~~~

My Mom & Stepdad, Adele and David Weitzel
who have always given their love and support

~~~

My dearly departed brother, John,
who is loved and missed each day

~~~

And to my wonderful and loving husband,
Scott,
and our sons, William & Eric,

who had patience when I was obsessed with writing,
gave me never-ending confidence and inspiration,
and for whom I am forever grateful
and blessed to have in my life.
I love you dearly.

~~~~~~~~~~~~~~~~~~~~~~~~~~~~~~

ALMOST HUMAN was originally published as a series of novels, now also broken into novellas as an alternate format. These are not stand-alone books - they are meant to be read in order, as the story unfolds chronologically.

ALMOST HUMAN ~ The First Series

FATAL INFATUATION
Part 1: Captivating Vampires
Part 2: Tempting Transgressions
Part 3: Venomous Revelations

LOST REFLECTIONS
Part 1: Persistent Persuasion
Part 2: Telling Tales
Part 3: Battles and Bliss

EVOLVING ECSTASY
Part 1: Ecstasy Unleashed
Part 2: Stakes and Sunshine
Part 3: Evolution of Love

ALMOST HUMAN ~ The Second Series

BORN TO BLOOD
Part 1: Vampiress Rising
Part 2: Exceeding Expectations
Part 3: Coping with Chaos
Part 4: Vampire Vertigo

DESCENDENT OF DARKNESS
Part 1: Determining Desires
Part 2: Undying Devotion
Part 3: Emotional Maelstrom
Part 4: Crossing the Line

Venomous Revelations

(Fatal Infatuation - Part 3)

Contents

Chapter 1 – Distraction

Felicity

The DownTime café and bookstore
7:45, Wednesday night

Felicity looked up from her register to see Allie enter the store. She had known that Alyson would inevitably show up, but she still had to stifle a groan upon seeing her actually arrive. She didn't want to have to socialize; she just wanted this night to be over. Not that her days were much better lately.

She had tried to keep busy, but still caught herself thinking of Cain sometimes. As bizarre as it might seem, she missed him. She'd find herself thinking of the endearing way he was always swiping the hair back from his face, or how the blue of his eyes seemed so deep and clear, almost iridescent; the rakish hint of a smile he would have, whenever he was teasing her.

Then she would have to stop and remind herself that he was not who she'd thought he was; to try and remember what he had done, without actually reliving it. It seemed almost like he was two different people: the Cain she had enjoyed spending time with and daydreamed about, and the vampire who had bitten her and stolen her blood.

Now, here came Alyson to remind her of him yet again. "Hey! Where's Cain?"

She sighed. Couldn't they just let her try to forget him? "He's not here."

"Well, the sun went down almost twenty minutes ago. How far away does he live?" Felicity just shook her head and looked up at the ceiling. Alyson continued with a mischievous smile. "Maybe he likes to have breakfast before coffee." Felicity opened her mouth in disgust. "Look at you all, shocked and astonished. He's a vampire, Felicity; he's got to drink blood sometime."

That was a disturbing thought. "But does he have to? I mean, couldn't he just...refrain?"

Allie chuckled. "Yeah, right, and how long could you abstain from eating?"

"But that's different, I'm alive. His body is, well... I just thought he could...do without, if he wanted," Felicity admitted.

"Sorry, sweetie, it doesn't work that way," Allie insisted.

"How do you know?"

"Trust me, he's drinkin' somethin'. He needs it. I think I'm gonna go pick on Ben for a while. He kind of expects it, and I'd hate to disappoint him," Allie said with a chuckle.

Felicity was still perplexed over the thought of Cain drinking someone's blood all this time, even before he'd bitten her. Somehow, she just thought that he could deny himself. And why did Allie just accept it so matter-of-factly? Didn't the thought even bother her? Maybe Alyson was wrong. Cain couldn't have been drinking people's blood all this time without her knowing, could he? Was she really so easy to deceive? How did Alyson get to be such an authority anyway?

Ah, well, at least it was just about time for her to leave. She went to find Ashley in the back of the store, shelving books. "I'm going to get ready to go."

"Oh, is it eight o'clock already?" Ashley asked.

"Almost, and I have friends coming to pick me up."

"Okay, I guess I'll see you in class Friday." Felicity turned to go when Ashley stopped her. "Hey Felicity, can I ask you something?"

"Sure, what?"

"You and Ben aren't...dating, are you?" Ashley asked hesitantly.

"No." Why did people keep asking her that?

"Oh, I was just wondering. Have you noticed anything wrong with him? He's been acting kind of weird lately."

"Weird how?"

"Well, I let him take me out last night, but he was like, all distracted and preoccupied. I was prepared to be very accommodating if you know what I mean, but he might as well not even have been there. He was very inattentive. That is so not like him, and I can't say I was very happy about it. He'd better step up and take a little better notice of me, or I might not let him take me to the dance on Saturday."

Felicity looked at her wearily. "Ashley, I am the last person you should be asking for insight on Ben. I don't know what is wrong with him, and frankly, I don't care. But I will say this: if I were you, I'd find another date for Homecoming. Goodnight."

She made her way reluctantly to the café and the employee lounge to retrieve her jacket and purse. Of course, there was no way to get behind the counter without seeing Ben. She had managed to avoid him for her entire shift. She hoped Karen would arrive on time and save her from having to sit out there and wait.

Alyson was sitting at the counter talking to Ben; they looked up as she arrived. Ben wore a dark expression. "So, do you think your fanged suitor will show up to escort you home?"

She ignored him and went into the back. As she was getting her stuff, Ben came and blocked the doorway. She looked up at him with annoyed impatience for a minute. He didn't move. "What do you want from me, Ben? What do you want me to say? Yes, I liked him, I admitted that to you. Now you're going to throw it in my face every chance you get? Grow up. I'm leaving. If Cain does show up, you can tell him that he missed me."

"Take it easy." She didn't reply. She made to push past him, but he caught her by the shoulders and forced her to look at him. She made him let go, but when she did look up into his face, she saw something there that had been missing for a while; that quiet concern that he used to have, when she had thought of him as her friend, back before his sole intent seemed to be harassing her for spending time with Cain and letting her know that he thought she was stupid for doing so.

He stared at her long and hard, seemingly trying to read the look in her eyes. She wondered how he would interpret what he saw there. The only feeling she was aware of was that of being exhausted by the whole damn thing. He spoke quietly and sincerely. "I'm sorry. I guess I haven't been much of a friend, huh? It's just hard to see someone you...care about, make the wrong choices."

She didn't even know what to say. She realized that he was trying to apologize, and yet she was outraged that he would presume to know what choices she'd made and whether or not they were correct by his standards! He may actually have been right, but he didn't know that, and she certainly wasn't planning on telling him.

She had the unreasonable urge to start crying because this was all just too much to deal with right now. She was just so fed up with everything, and she felt like she just had to get out of here before Cain did decide to pay her a visit. As if right on cue, she heard Karen out in the café talking to Alyson. "I have to go."

Ben seemed a little hurt that she wouldn't stay and talk to him. Then he heard Alyson call Felicity from out in the café. He stepped aside, and she walked past him to the waiting girls.

Karen saw her and waved. "Hi! Ready to go? The guys are waiting in the car."

Felicity noticed Allie and Ben exchange a puzzled look at the word 'guys'. "Yeah, let's get out of here."

Alyson looked confused. "Aren't you going to wait and see if Cain shows up?"

"I'm sure you'll tell me all about it tomorrow if he does."

Felicity walked out and stood waiting just outside the door. Karen said her goodbyes and followed, passing and then leading her out to a waiting car, a nice new four-door sedan, dark blue. She saw Jack and a guy who could only be Todd, sitting up front. She and Karen climbed into the back.

Karen had spoken truly; Todd was accurately described as 'cute'. He had very curly light brown hair and an honest and sweet face. Introductions were made, and they headed off to the movie theater. Felicity sat silently in the back after a few initial polite comments. She hoped she didn't seem rude, but she really didn't feel like talking.

As they neared the theater, she began to feel warm and flushed, as though she had drunk a few glasses of wine, although of course, she'd had nothing. As they pulled into the lot, she really felt quite odd. Like she had alternating hot flashes and chills. Was she nearing a nervous breakdown, or coming down with the flu? Wouldn't that just be perfect?

As they left the car, she forced herself to smile at Todd. She tried her very best to radiate accepting and friendly vibes toward him and make him feel confident. They all bought tickets, popcorn, and sodas. She paid for her own, and they made their way to their theater.

They found seats and Felicity took off her jacket, settling herself in the aisle seat next to Todd. They made small talk until the lights dimmed and then sat back to watch the movie; Felicity found she couldn't concentrate, though.

Her hot flashes and chills had turned into a sort of tingling feeling. She felt so odd. It was almost like...static electricity. She had heard somewhere that people who are about to get struck by lightning could feel it before it actually struck; something about the way the particles of their bodies became charged and their hair stood on end. Well, her hair wasn't raised, and she highly doubted she would be struck by lightning in the movie theater, but that was the thought this strange sensation brought to mind. She felt...charged, expectant. It was so weird. It had nothing to do with Todd, she was sure. He was very nice, but she didn't imagine there would be any sort of chemistry between them.

For some reason, Cain kept coming to mind. Something about how she felt now that reminded her of the way she had felt when he had bitten her. No matter how she tried to block that from her mind, she just couldn't help but face the truth. It had been an amazingly intimate experience. Just a vague flash of it through her mind could make her shiver. As she thought of it now, she had the inexplicable urge to go to him. As if she needed to experience it again. She fought it back with a chill.

She couldn't say why this odd feeling would remind her of that. Maybe it was just the fact that both feelings were so far removed from anything else that she had ever known, but she had to admit that she suddenly realized how much she missed Cain. She did feel a terrible urge to see him, however unreasonable that might be.

She couldn't help but ponder what Allie had said about Cain needing to drink blood. She felt rather foolish about it, really. Of course, a vampire needed to drink blood; that was a given. But somehow, when she had first discovered that he was a vampire, he had put her under the impression that he could do without.

What had he said, really? She thought back carefully. He'd never said that he didn't drink blood; he said he didn't hurt people. That gave her a chill, because he had drunk from her, and although she had felt many indescribable things, she knew full well that it hadn't really hurt. There'd been an instant of pain when his fangs had first pierced her flesh, but she'd hardly had time to recognize it before it was soothed by other feelings. Even Allie had said it didn't hurt when she had been bitten. Did Cain mean that he drank, but didn't kill people?

That thought produced an inexplicable wave of what she could only identify as jealousy, as bewildering as that may be. She actually felt jealous at the thought of him engaging in the act of drinking blood from someone else, the way that he had from her! What was wrong with her? That was insane!

She had the bizarre mental image of Cain standing before a crowd of girls looking for an intended victim, and all of them raising their hands and screaming, 'Pick me, pick me!'. Why didn't she just go into the bathroom, slit her wrists, and be done with it? She really must be losing her mind!

Felicity realized she must have been fidgeting, because Todd looked over a couple of times, as if trying to figure out why she was so uncomfortable. She made herself sit still and stare at the screen. Still, she couldn't pay attention. Cain kept invading her thoughts as though he were sitting right next to her. She almost felt as if she had a slight 'pins and needles' sensation traveling over her whole body.

For some reason, she began thinking about the night Cain had given her the vial of his blood. More precisely, the kiss they had shared. She kept remembering how passionate it had been, and how it had seemed to almost produce a pleasant sort of 'high' in her.

Her mind was probably embellishing the memory to be more than it really was, but it did make her wish that he were a regular guy, so that things could be different between them. She certainly wouldn't mind a few more kisses like that! She even found herself closing her eyes and reliving the kiss in her mind. Stop that! she silently reprimanded herself. He is not somebody to be fantasizing about!

Why had he given her that vial anyway, if not to protect her? Why would he do that if he had been planning all along to hurt her? As mixed up as her feelings about the event might be, she still had to consider someone drinking her blood as harmful. Harming her couldn't have been his intention, not from the beginning anyway. She wondered if he'd changed his mind.

The evening passed, and the movie finally came to an end. Someone suggested they go for coffee and ice cream. Felicity suffered herself to be brought along, and she hoped no one would want to discuss the film. She hadn't really paid a bit of mind to it.

The one thing she was grateful for was the fact that, as they left the theater, that odd feeling that had persisted all evening finally began to fade. By the time they reached the diner, it was all but gone. Todd seemed a bit distracted, and she imagined he was thinking about his ex-girlfriend. She herself almost choked over ordering when she saw 'Butter Rum Ripple' on the ice cream menu. She ordered Black Cherry instead. She still had a hard time eating it.

As the evening came to an end, they headed back to the dorms. Felicity had thought the guys would just drop them off at the door, but Jack insisted that they walk the girls inside.

Karen let them in with her key, and she and Jack went off down the hall to her room for a more private goodbye, leaving Todd and Felicity standing alone in the front parlor. No one else was around. How awkward. What was she supposed to say to this guy? She felt bad; she had hardly even looked at him since the movie theater. She hoped he didn't take it personally.

"I had a really nice time," she told him; a harmless exaggeration.

He smiled. "No, you didn't. It's okay, I know I'm not great company lately. I've kind of had a lot on my mind. Not a great first impression, I know, but thanks for coming."

"You were fine company; my head wasn't there. I've kind of got a lot going on, too."

"Well, here's a crazy idea. Since neither one of us seems ready to commit our attention fully to someone else right now, well, were you going to the Homecoming dance with anyone? 'Cause if you weren't, but you'd like to go...maybe we could go together. You know, and ignore each other in a more formal setting."

She had to laugh. He was sweet. "I don't know. I wasn't even going to go."

"Well, it's okay if you don't want to. I just thought I'd ask. Considering the dance is only three nights away and I don't have a date, I wasn't going either, but it wouldn't have to be like a real date, if you don't want. I mean, we could just go and keep each other company."

Felicity reconsidered. Why was she saying no anyway? Just because she wouldn't be seeing Cain anymore, why should she stay home? Maybe this was just what she needed. "Well...okay, I'll go."

"Really, you want to?" he asked hopefully.

"Why not? What am I going to do, sit in my room all night?"

"It'll be fun," Todd assured her.

"I don't really dance though," she admitted, apologetically.

"I'm sure we can work around the actual dancing part."

"Cool. Oh, I'm working until ten o'clock. Sorry, I know the dance starts at nine."

"That's alright, we'll make an entrance. Should I meet you here?"

She froze for a moment in indecision. What would be worse, walking home alone, or chancing seeing Cain with Todd around? "No, um, would you mind picking me up at work?"

"Don't you want to come home to change first?"

"I know, it seems weird, but I don't like to leave work alone, if you don't mind. I can get ready there."

"Okay, whatever you want. I'll be there at ten."

"Thanks. I'll see you Saturday."

"Great, I'll see you then. Goodnight."

"Goodnight, it was nice meeting you," she called after him with a wave, as he walked out the door. She headed up the stairs as Jack came into the parlor from down the hall. He didn't notice her on the stairs and went straight out. She went up to her room to get ready for bed.

What was she doing, going to the dance with Todd? Didn't she have enough people to worry about, without adding someone else into the mix? Why was she feeling so out of sorts tonight? The whole movie theater experience had left her feeling all flustered.

As she got beneath the covers and switched off the lights, thoughts of Cain once again tried to invade her mind. She was so tired and weary of fighting them, she didn't even try. She just closed her eyes and let them carry her off to sleep.

~~~~~~~~~~~~~~~~~~~~~~~~~~~~~~~~~~~~

Felicity awoke to a knock at her door. She found herself opening it before she was even fully awake. She looked up groggily and froze in shock...it was Cain.

She stood there, in her short little nightgown, her hair mussed from sleep and her heart suddenly pounding so loudly she was sure he could hear it. She moistened her lips but couldn't manage to speak.

Something in the back of her mind was trying to tell her that she was supposed to be afraid of him. He was a vampire. He had bitten her. He was so handsome...

He wore a sad, little apologetic look upon his face that completely disarmed her. He didn't seem threatening in the least. She looked into his deep blue eyes and saw nothing but kindness, comfort, and a plea for forgiveness.

He spoke quietly and sincerely. "I'm sorry I woke you, but I just had to see you." She just stood there, staring at him in indecisive struggle. "Please trust that I would never hurt you. I just want to talk. Can I come in?"

A million responses flitted through her befuddled mind. She should be angry with him. She should be scared of him. He had told her before that he wouldn't hurt her, right before he had bitten her, but it hadn't actually...hurt.

If she were smart, she would slam the door in his face. She knew she would never do that, though. She should, at the very least, tell him that he had violated her trust and had no right to come expecting her to forgive him, but the only words she found herself uttering were "Come in."

She moved like a sleepwalker, dreamy and dazed as she sat down on the bed. He entered and closed the door behind him. The reading lamp by her bed lit the room with a dim glow, although she didn't remember turning it on. He came to stand before her and took her hand from her lap, raising it to his lips for a small kiss that melted her heart.

He sat down next to her on the bed, still holding her hand in his own. "I am so sorry for my transgression. You're just so irresistible to me. Try as I might, I am completely overwhelmed by your beauty and drawn to your tender soul." His words gave her joyous chills, and she sat in mute wonder, taking in the earnestness of his gaze. "I know I have no right to expect your forgiveness, but please, if you can at all find it in your heart to accept my apology, it would mean the world to me."

It seemed all the things that she would want to hear…

He continued. "I've existed with such darkness hovering over me for so long, and you are like light incarnate. I am falling helplessly in love with you, Felicity."

She sat staring into his eyes for a few more moments before she realized that he was waiting for a response. "I forgive you," she breathed.

She could swear there were tears in his eyes as he gave her a relieved smile and squeezed her hand in both of his own. "Thank you."

"You're in love with me?" she whispered, bewilderedly.

"Helplessly."

She shook her head in disbelief. "You're a vampire. I'm the one who's helpless here."

"I won't take your blood again," he promised, "but I might steal a kiss." He slowly leaned forward to do just that. It was a soft yet sensual touch of the lips; hesitant, seeking her approval. The cherished memory of the first true kiss they had shared surfaced, and she knew that she just had to kiss him deeper and experience that euphoria again. She was about to bring her arms up around him to do just that when he ended the kiss and leaned back from her.

Even without taking things further, her head was already spinning. Everything in the room had such a hazy, dreamlike quality to it. Only Cain was sharp and clear to her focus. "Is this real?" she asked him in wonder.

"What I feel for you is real," he assured her. Her eyes widened as she dared to believe he could be speaking the truth. He gave her a little nod. "I can't tell you how badly I want you right now," he confided in a whisper.

"Then don't tell me, show me," she begged him, breathlessly.

He shook his head a bit, as though reluctant to act on his desires. "I try so hard to keep myself under control, even in this, but I'm like a dam holding back the ocean here. Are you sure that's a force you want unleashed?"

Felicity held his gaze steady with her own. "Drown me."

He took her into his arms, and their lips reunited in sensual bliss. As her tongue danced with his, his hands caressed her lower back, sending shivers through her. The kiss seemed to go on forever as the enchanting sense of lightheaded pleasure came back to her from the first kiss they had shared. It was just as she had remembered, and then it became more. Intense and filled with powerful emotion, he kissed her, still as he lay her back on the bed.

He finally released her mouth as she gasped for air, and his lips traveled down her throat. She froze for a moment, but he never paused as he moved down her body, bestowing kisses through her thin nightgown along the way.

He pushed up the material to expose her hips, her belly, and then her breasts. He found her right nipple with his tongue, and after a few teasing flicks, he took it into his mouth to suckle. A gasping moan caught in her throat as he ran his hand up the inside of her thigh. He gently eased aside her panties, and his finger found her slick with wanting him.

She suddenly realized that it was his bare chest, muscular, smooth, and cool, that lay against her stomach and thighs, although she couldn't remember him undressing.

He came back to kiss her again, although his hand continued to make her writhe and squirm as it explored the depths between her legs. She fondled the strong curve of his shoulder with her hand and then ran it down his back to find the soft swell of his ass. She gave it an appreciative squeeze and then dared to let her hand travel around his thigh to find his erection, hard and waiting for her.

The moan that rumbled from his throat was almost identical to the one he had uttered when he had tasted her blood. She stroked and squeezed him gently and then firmly until he forcefully broke from their kiss to remove her hand. He brought her wrists above her head in his own as he parted her thighs with his knee.

She was thrilled but nervous with anticipation as she awaited the thrust that she had only dreamed of but never experienced. She felt him hard and ready, gently pushing at her opening when, with a strong and final motion, he entered her.

Ecstasy.

Her fears quickly fled as she felt him fill her body with his own, deep inside her like a missing piece to make her complete. She reveled in the rapture of it, but then had to suck in a breath of shock as he began to move. Slowly at first, but then stronger and faster, he thrust himself into her again and again. Each pushing and pulling movement brought tingling waves of pleasure that finally exploded within her in a rhapsody of gratification.

Felicity sat up with a gasp.

The room was dark and empty of anyone but her; silent, except for her own rapid breathing. She was alone.

It was just a dream; a vivid, sensual, achingly real dream. She closed her eyes for a moment, trying to recapture the sensation, unlike anything she had ever known. Past experiences with boys back home hadn't been nearly as exciting and were anything but romantic. She'd had some fanciful daydreams and tried to imagine what it would be like to love a man, but never anything so immersive as this!

No man had ever awakened such avid desire in her before. She'd never actually met someone worthy of such a fantasy. Knowing what her real kiss with Cain had been like, she had no doubt that he could turn such a fantasy into reality for her.

Then she opened her eyes again with a mental reprimand. You aren't supposed to be dreaming about him! She reached up to find the place where he had bitten her throat. The warm and tingling sensations caused by touching the spot were much faded and more relived in her memory than on her skin, but still brought back waves of ecstasy to her recollection.

She withdrew her hand and shook her head, trying to clear herself of the thoughts. He's no good for you. Think of something else, she chided herself as she lay her head back on the pillow, but as she closed her eyes again to try to sleep, she couldn't help but hope for more dreams.

~~~~~~~~~~~~~~~~~~~~~~~~~~~~~~

Thursday morning was a blur of struggle between guilt and daydreams. By lunchtime, however, she decided that although fantasies were fun, reality was completely different. She could not let silly imaginings compromise her common sense. Cain was a vampire. He had bitten her and drunk her blood, and no matter how handsome, she had to consider him dangerous. She would do her best to chase thoughts of him from her mind and focus on anything other than vampires.

Not that she was likely to be able to dodge the subject around Ben and Allie. She planned on taking lunch up to her room to avoid them, but Ben found her just outside the cafeteria. She thought of trying to pretend she hadn't seen him, but he wasn't going to let her.

"Liss!" Ben was the only one who ever called her that. Originally, she had kind of liked it. Now she thought of asking him not to, but it seemed pointless and hurtful. He caught up to her. "Hi. Can we sit and talk?"

"Why, have you thought of something else you could say to upset me?"

"I wasn't trying to upset you," he said quietly.

"Right, because calling me stupid, questioning my virtue, and letting me know that you would like to see someone that you think I care about get killed, shouldn't upset me?"

"Okay, so maybe I was trying a little, but I had good intentions."

She raised her eyebrows at him and then shook her head dismissively. "Whatever, Ben, I don't even want to know. I'm going to go get some lunch." He followed her to the lunch line.

"You know I consider you a close friend, don't you?"

She looked at him as if he were nuts. "Is that why I get such special treatment?"

"Yes, because my friends are supposed to know better than to get involved with...the wrong kinds of people," he said, glancing around at all of the potential eavesdroppers on the line.

She stopped to stare at him intensely for a moment. No, there was no way that he knew what had happened between her and Cain. "Well, big brother, you can happily consider me uninvolved," she said, as she moved her tray along and selected a chef's salad from the case.

Ben looked unsure whether or not to be pleased with himself. Like maybe she was just trying to pacify him. "Good. What, did you two have a little spat or something?" he asked skeptically.

"Something like that."

Ben grabbed a sandwich from the case, and they moved on. "Well, it's for the best. You know that, right? And don't call me 'big brother'." They got drinks and paid for their selections. "There's Allie," Ben said, waving across the room.

"Oh, good," she replied with a sarcastic lilt.

Ben stopped to give her a wounded look. "Don't you like Allie? I thought you guys were getting along."

"Well, you have to admit, she does take some getting used to, but yeah, she's okay. It's just that vampires seem to be her choice subject, and they're not my favorite topic these days."

"So, we'll talk about something else."

They reached the table and sat down as Allie greeted them. "Hi! So, Cain never showed last night."

Ben and Felicity shared a glance. Ben answered her. "Yeah, I guess he and Felicity aren't as close as I thought."

Alyson gave Felicity a curious look. "So, nobody knows what he and Arif talked about? Well, maybe he'll come see you tonight."

"I'm not working tonight," Felicity told her with a shrug.

"Neither am I," Ben admitted.

Allie knitted her brows and muttered, "Damn. Well, I am. Sometimes he comes into Tommy's, maybe I'll see him."

Ben shook his head disapprovingly. "Alyson, haven't you ever heard the expression 'curiosity killed the cat'?"

Allie smiled. "Cain's the one who's a big pussy cat. He wouldn't bite me." She seemed to watch a little too closely as Felicity flinched. "I'm gonna ask him what happened."

"I should know better than to try and caution you by now. Anyway," he looked over at Felicity, who had been quietly picking at her salad, "I'm sick of vampires. Let's talk about something else."

Allie flashed an impish grin at him. "Okay, stud. So, who are you takin' to the dance?" Ben rolled his eyes. "Come on, it's a little late to be leavin' people hangin'."

Ben looked up at her and answered quietly. "I already asked Brenda yesterday."

"Does Ashley know that?"

He shrugged. "I was going to say something last night, but you know, I never actually asked Ashley. Why should I feel responsible for what she might have assumed?" Alyson gave him a look of disapproval. "I'll talk to her tonight. What if she really did think I'd take her? I hope she won't be mad. Do you think she'll have time to find another date?"

Allie giggled. "Don't worry, Ben. I'm sure she's got a whole bunch of hunks just lined up and waiting to make you jealous."

"I can hardly wait," he answered dryly. "Am I buying you a ticket again?"

"I don't think I'm gonna go this year," Allie told him.

"Allie, you always go to everything," Ben insisted.

"I know, but I'm kind of between boyfriends right now. And you're gonna be all over Brenda, so I'll have no one to dance with."

Ben looked over to Felicity. "You should go with 'Liss. You guys can check out all of those 'college hotties' she was telling you about."

"I already have a date," Felicity said timidly.

Ben was taken aback. Allie smiled. "You do?" they asked.

"Yes," she answered quietly. She cut off Allie's obvious question before she could even ask it. "He's human. Why do you guys seem so shocked? You don't think I could attract a normal guy?"

Ben looked properly abashed. "No, of course not. I mean, of course you could. You're...very attractive. You just never mentioned anyone."

"His name's Todd," Felicity supplied.

"Oh. Then, I guess I'll see you there," Ben said thoughtfully.

"I guess," she said with a shrug.

Alyson sat back and pouted. "Maybe I should ask somebody. I don't want to be the only one not going, but I'm certainly not going to hang around as the fifth wheel either."

Ben fixed her with an odd look. "Allie, you don't even go to this school. I know we usually go to stuff together, but it's not a big deal."

"Maybe I'll just go to the bonfire," Allie said thoughtfully.

"What's that?" Felicity asked.

Ben answered. "It's a school tradition. They have this big bonfire before the dance. It's supposed to signify roasting the other team or something. It's pretty barbaric if you think about it."

"Oh. Well, I'm working until ten, so we'll just be going to the dance," Felicity told them.

"That sucks," Allie interjected. "Couldn't you switch with someone?"

"I don't mind. We'll just go late," Felicity assured her.

Ben sat up and gathered his stuff. "Speaking of late, it's time to go or I will be." He glanced at Allie. "Maybe I'll stop into Tommy's later, just to make sure you stay out of trouble."

"Like having you around ever stopped me," Allie told him with a smirk.

"Well, God knows what you do when I'm not there."

Allie laughed. "Don't you wish you knew?"

"Not really. Sometimes ignorance is bliss." He turned to Felicity, who was also getting ready to leave. "I'll see you tomorrow night."

"What's tomorrow night?" she asked in surprise.

"We're closing together," he reminded her.

"Oh. Guess I'll see you then, bye." She left for class, wondering if she'd done the right thing, accepting Todd's invitation to the dance. It was nice being able to say she had a date, but it wasn't like she was expecting anything to come of it.

At least Todd hadn't seemed too disillusioned either. They were just going to get out and keep each other company - no strings or expectations. Did he really believe that, or was he just trying to get her to go? Oh well, it didn't matter. They'd hang out at the dance together and see what happened. Maybe she'd end up liking him more than she thought...if she could just get Cain out of her head.

Chapter 2 - Enduring

Cain

The movie theater
Thursday night

Cain sat in the movie theater and tried to pay attention to the show, again. He could hardly believe his bad luck last night. He had come all the way to the theater to try and keep himself away from Felicity, and she had followed him to the very building.

Of course, she'd had no idea that he was there. He had felt her approaching when she'd entered the furthest extent of his range of perception, which was roughly a mile. It was just before the movie started, he had felt her trace flicker into his mind with a delighted sort of ache; a sudden reminder of her and the intimacy that they had shared.

He had closed his eyes and reveled in her light, but had also reluctantly hoped that she would not come too close. Of course, she had. As the distance had closed, he had felt her glow strengthen in his mind and become more.

He'd been grateful that she hadn't chosen the same room where he sat, but he could feel her through the wall as though she were mere inches away.

He'd closed his eyes and felt himself enveloped in her presence. His blood had practically sung with the knowledge of her proximity. He'd wondered if she felt him. She should, but she wouldn't understand. He'd thought of leaving, so as not to disturb her, but he hadn't been able to force himself from his seat. It had been a struggle just to keep from going to find her, an endless torture. Nearly two hours of feeling her nearness, but not being able to look upon her, to touch her, to try to explain.

He had seriously considered going to her, taking her from her seat, and rushing her to a quiet corner where they could talk, but what if she were afraid of him and caused a scene? And of course, she would not have come alone. That had brought about an unwelcome wave of irritation. Who had she come with? Alyson hadn't been there. Her mark from Sindy was just about gone, but he was fairly sure he would still see it if he concentrated. He didn't know who else Felicity usually socialized with, other than Ben. Did it matter? It was only a movie, but someone else had the pleasure of her company while he was denied.

He remembered how he'd gripped the armrests of his seat with all of his strength and forced stillness upon himself. It had been a long time since he'd had to fight so hard against his instincts. Other than...stopping himself from drinking from her. No, he shouldn't even think of it. He could not allow himself to relive that experience while in such a fragile state. He needed to keep himself separate from her; give himself another night or two.

His body's reaction to her nearness had shown him that he wasn't ready. If he could be assured of her acceptance, it wouldn't matter. In a positive circumstance, he was sure he could handle himself, but for her to deny him while his body needed her so badly could turn dangerous. His will was strong, but he didn't care to test it. Just another night or two, and he would have full control again.

His movie had ended, and people had begun to leave, but he hadn't dared to move. Surely, she would be leaving soon as well. She had arrived when his own film was only just starting; better to wait her out than to chance her seeing him.

He hadn't planned on actually leaving the theater, but to stay for another picture, and he couldn't chance hanging about in the lobby while she was here. He'd watched the credits roll as people moved around him to the exit. Finally, theater employees had come to collect popcorn buckets and sweep the floor.

A young girl in a red and white striped vest had come to tell him that he must leave before the next showing. He'd assured her that he only needed a moment more to rest; to please excuse him, as he was not feeling well. She'd left him alone, but he'd known she was only going to find someone else to make him leave.

Somehow, he'd endured until he felt Felicity move from the theater. It was almost painful to feel her recede, but the practical side of him was very relieved. When he had been certain that she had left the building, he'd made his way out into the lobby and sat on a bench near the bathrooms. He'd followed her in his mind's eye until she became indistinct and then…she was gone.

He'd spent the rest of the night in the theater, almost afraid to let himself leave, until they closed. Finally, he'd gone home, not having to pass the dorms, for which he was very grateful. For the most part, he was glad because he hadn't wanted to tease himself with her presence again, but a small part of him was actually afraid to pass those dorms and feel that she wasn't there.

If that had happened, he would not have been able to rest until he'd searched for and found her. And if she wasn't in her room by this time of night, it would be much safer for all involved if he did not find where she was. So, he'd gone home, safely out of her range, and tried to read until morning.

Now here he was again, at the theater, prepared to sit and watch the rest of the films that he had not yet seen, and even those he had again if necessary. Anything to keep himself occupied. He felt secure in the fact that she would not come back so soon. He did find it curious, though, that he hadn't felt the presence of any other vampires. Where were they all?

Was Arif keeping them out of his way, or cloaking them? He was unsure what to make of the man, and that worried him. He was unlike most vampires Cain had known. A creature like Sindy might do something surprising from time to time, but basically, he knew what to expect from her and not to trust her.

He had not met many vampires that were past the century mark in their lives, which Arif surely was. Most old ones were either outwardly hostile or shy and reluctant to even speak with others.

Arif had said that he'd brought his own blood supply, so he had no need to hunt the vicinity. Cain had met other, younger vampires who followed the practice of keeping a 'stable' or a 'harem', but they usually did not have much patience for Cain's advice. He disagreed with their ways and had never spent enough time in their company to really know them. This, in turn, meant that he couldn't really speculate on what to expect of one like them, like Arif.

Some vampires came to realize that it was a large risk to prey upon humans night after night, even if they didn't kill, but they were unwilling or uneducated in relying on animal blood for their existence, as Cain did. So, they would collect a 'stable' of about a half dozen humans, sometimes called 'pets', to visit repeatedly or keep in their constant care. They would alternate drinking from these, so as to never fully deplete their supply.

Repeat visits to a victim were, of course, risky in their own right if not properly handled. Most vampires opted to keep their humans secluded from the rest of society. Sometimes they were kept by force, but usually a smart vampire would choose drug addicts who could be kept deliriously high and oblivious to their plight. Whether the vampire realized it at the outset or learned through experience, the venom they administered with each bite also helped to control them.

Cain had heard rumors of vampires who would steal young children and then raise them to be kept, showering them with material things and keeping them secluded from the outside world. These pets were like so many spoiled rich children as they matured, being allowed to party and play with others at nightclubs and such, to a certain extent, and always under a watchful eye. They knew nothing of responsibility other than feeding and pleasing their master.

Once in a while, one could even find a human who was happy to be kept, for reasons of their own. They were content to live in a sort of symbiotic relationship with a vampire who would provide for their needs. But that was usually not the case. Usually, a combination of addiction and force prevailed, and whether they realized it or not, those kept were prisoners. That entire arrangement was not something Cain was comfortable accepting.

Along the same lines, sometimes a 'guard' would be kept as well. This was similar to Sindy's practices; although whether she had picked it up from Arif or stumbled upon it on her own, he couldn't say.

A vampire might sire other, lesser vampires to do their bidding. They were purposely not made well enough for true independent thinking and then used for protection, sex, or however their sire saw fit. Of course, in Sindy's case, the quality of her 'work' was more through incompetence than any purposeful plan, but they served her all the same.

He wondered what Sindy had thought of Arif's meeting with Cain. She had to have questioned Arif over it. She would know that Felicity was now marked and therefore, not to be touched. He also wondered if Arif would mention anything about Ben.

Cain had entertained the thought earlier this evening of finding Ben to tell him that Sindy wanted him, to give him warning. He had approached the DownTime and seen that Ben was not there. He had felt that Felicity was in the dorms and was glad to let her be. He was content that at least he knew where she was, but that did not help him find Ben. He certainly wasn't going to go and knock on Felicity's door to see if he was there.

He supposed that if he really wanted to, he could leave a message for him with Alyson, over at Tommy's, but although he could indeed, faintly sense Alyson's presence there, the last thing he wanted to do right now was enter the bar.

He still felt a little jittery to have Felicity close again. He didn't want to have to talk to anyone; he really just wanted to go off on his own. Ben could fend for himself for a day or two without Cain's advice. Ben was used to looking out for vampires anyway, so it shouldn't make any difference.

So, he found himself back at the movies again. He briefly wondered how many movies he had seen throughout his lifetime. Probably thousands. Just another night, he kept telling himself. Just make it through another night.

Chapter 3 – Look at you!

Felicity

The DownTime café and bookstore
9:45, Friday night

It was almost time to close, and still no sign of Cain. Felicity was quietly relieved, but had to admit, she was starting to stress a little from the tension.

She'd spent last night alone in her room, catching up on homework. She'd also spoken aloud as many phrases as she could think of, all with the sole purpose of trying to un-invite Cain from her room. She wasn't sure if they would work, and she didn't really expect him to come anyway…but it couldn't hurt.

She did assume she would see him tonight, though. He hadn't been to the DownTime in a while; it was very unlike him. Was he deliberately avoiding her? He must be, but why?

If he was going to attack her, she almost wished he'd get it over with. This anticipation and not knowing what he would do was driving her crazy. Exactly what had happened the night that he'd bitten her? Had he simply lost control, or was it something that he had planned to do all along?

Her instincts kept swinging her back and forth over the issue. First, she would tell herself that she could not possibly have read every single gesture of his wrongly. She couldn't be that gullible. He really had cared for her, genuinely.

Then she would tell herself that she could not judge him by her own standards, because he was not human. Her own methods of reading people's intentions did not apply. He was a totally alien entity that she could not understand, and therefore, he was dangerous. She couldn't hope to guess his agenda. She wished he would make some sort of move, so she would know what to think.

As things stood now, she was frightened by what had happened, but with a few nights of distance, she had a hard time thinking of him in person as someone to be afraid of, but was that only a residual feeling spurred on by her dreams? If he violently attacked her and turned out to be a truly evil monster, at least she would know that she'd been deceived. Right now, the fact that he had bitten her just didn't fit with the rest of her feelings towards him. It was very unsettling.

Alyson was there again and was quite vocal about her disappointment over yet another wasted evening and her unrequited curiosity. She had been very annoyed that Cain had not come into Tommy's again. Now she was pacing the café and driving Ben nuts. Felicity was glad she had been able to spend most of her evening hiding away in the back of the bookstore, so as to avoid hearing her complaints.

There were no customers, so she began her closing routine a little early. Now, as she closed out her register, Allie came over to bug her for a while, so Ben could mop the floor. "Why hasn't he come? Did you tell him not to?"

"No. I haven't even seen him," Felicity answered.

"Then where is he? From what you said, there are just too many damn vampires in this town right now. That makes things really unsafe."

Felicity stopped counting her register to give Allie a perplexed look. "Are you worried about Cain?"

Alyson looked confused for a moment. "No. It's not safe for anyone. I just know that vampires don't usually gather in such large numbers unless it means big trouble. They really don't play well together, you know? So, this is really weird, and it sounds like something dangerous is going on. If so, I wanna know about it. And right now, Cain is the only vampire around here that might actually tell me."

"Well, sorry, but I don't think he's coming."

Allie looked at her for a very long time. Then she walked back over to the café, tiptoeing over the wet floor, perched on a bar stool, and slumped over the counter. She raked her fingers through her hair in exasperation. "This sucks!"

Felicity finished her register and went over to join Allie at the counter. Ben came out from the back. "Hey, maybe we can get out of here early tonight. Go flip the sign for me," he said to Felicity, pointing at the open/closed sign on the door. As he did, his face suddenly went pale. Felicity and Alyson noticed his expression and turned to look as they heard the little bell ring over the door.

Sindy entered the store. She strolled in wearing a sweet smile, as if she hadn't a care in the world. Her grin grew broader as she witnessed the three of them at the counter. Felicity and Allie had stood from their stools. Ben slowly came out from behind the counter; it was he who found his voice first. "Get out."

Sindy acted as though he hadn't said a word. "Well, looky, looky, the gang's all here. Guess I picked a good night to come visit," she said, stopping on the carpet, just short of the café entrance.

Just then, Alyson seemed to break free of the paralysis that had held her. "Come to get your ass kicked again?" she asked, as she tried to lunge at Sindy.

Luckily, Ben had foreseen her intention and lurched forward to grab her in a sort of hug from behind. Alyson's feet slid around on the wet floor, and she was unable to get any leverage to make Ben let go. Ben widened his stance and managed to hold her while still keeping his feet.

Sindy smiled maliciously. "Hold her tight, Ben. I've got friends outside." She took a step closer and gazed at Allie. "As much as I should take this opportunity to put you back in your place, I won't. Although less witnesses means that I could have a lot more fun but, another time. You really aren't the one that I came here to see." She looked around a little, sizing up the place. "So, this is Cain's beloved sanctuary. It's funny that he's the only one not here. Do you know why? I'll bet I do."

Ben still held Allie, although she seemed to have calmed down, while watching Sindy intently. "What the hell do you want?" Ben asked.

Sindy shook her head as if in regret. "Oh, Ben, don't be disappointed, but I'm not here to see you either. Our time will come, I promise, but for you, I want to plan something special. You're just too good to rush."

Ben looked like he had planned to say something, but Alyson started cursing and struggling with renewed fury, and he was taken with holding her back. Sindy laughed. "But you know, while I have your attention, I should ask you something. I know the college is having the Homecoming dance tomorrow. I don't suppose you need a date?"

This so caught them off guard that Ben let go of Allie, who immediately burst out laughing. "You have got to be kidding," Ben stated in shock.

Allie tried to rein in her laughter to answer. "Actually, you're a little late; he already has two. Ben, you've become quite the magnet, haven't you? Even the dead girls wanna play."

Sindy looked amused. "Two dates? Well, aren't you the virile young buck? I'll try to make sure none of that gets lost in the process."

Allie stepped forward and made to grab for Sindy, whose eyes flashed red momentarily as she took a step back. Ben held the back of Allie's shirt and gave her a reminding tug. Sindy smiled and continued. "Don't try to tell me you haven't fantasized about us, Ben."

"Actually, Sindy, I have. You and me, outside on the grass, watching the sunrise."

He had her going for a second, but her surprise quickly turned to annoyance. "You're so cute; I am really going to enjoy claiming you. Save me a dance." She held up a hand to silence them. "But you have to stop distracting me."

She turned her eyes to Felicity, and her smile positively beamed. "Because here is what I came to see. Look at you! I can't believe it! I had to come and see you for myself!" She stepped closer to Felicity, who edged back towards Ben and Allie.

Sindy's voice took on a soft and soothing quality. "It's okay, sweetie, you don't have to be afraid of me anymore. You've got big, strong Cain to take care of you now, don't you?" She dropped her voice to a whisper. "Or maybe Cain is the one you should be afraid of."

Felicity froze like a deer in headlights. It was Alyson who yelled, "That's enough bitch. You'd better head for that door, because if you don't, your friends will only be here in time to watch you turn to dust."

Sindy seemed unconcerned. "Relax, I'm going. I've seen what I came to see." She leaned a little closer to Felicity to whisper, "I'll bet he's got a nice touch. Enjoy it while you can." Alyson moved towards her, but she was already heading out the door. Allie followed her and locked it.

Ben took a deep breath and looked at them in confusion. "What the hell was that all about?"

Alyson turned from watching Sindy leave through the glass of the door. "I guess she was feeling nostalgic and wanted a second date."

"A second date?" Felicity questioned.

Allie laughed. "Back in tenth grade, Ben took her to the high school Homecoming dance."

Felicity turned to look at Ben. He was staring at her strangely. "She was human then," he explained distractedly. "That's not what I meant. The stuff she said about you and Cain. What was that?"

Felicity gave her head a little shake. Obviously, Sindy must know that Cain had bitten her, but she didn't understand how. She certainly wasn't going to tell Ben that.

Allie strode purposely forward to Ben and took him by the arm, back to the counter. "Who knows? Crazy witch. Finish your stuff so we can get out of here." She glanced back towards the door, and Felicity, who began to realize that Allie might not be quite as clueless as she sometimes affected.

Felicity handed Ben her locker key. He was about to say something to her when Allie spoke again. "Looks like you've got your own personal stalker. Worried?"

"It's nothing new. Sindy's tried for me before. I'll just have to be very careful, that's all."

"Do you think she'll go to the dance?"

Now Ben looked worried. "God, I hope not, but I bet she will. And I do not have two dates, by the way. I talked to Ashley; she knows I'm going with Brenda."

"How'd she take it?"

"She acted like she didn't expect me to take her anyway, and said she had another date already. I don't know if that was true, but it works for me." Ben finished the last details, and they headed for the door.

Felicity looked out into the dark. "Do you think they're waiting for us?"

Ben pulled out his cross from somewhere and handed Allie his stake. He looked to Felicity, who, in turn, reluctantly pulled her own stake from her purse. "We'll see," Ben said.

As Ben got out his keys, Allie turned to Felicity. "Don't worry, you'll be okay," she said quietly.

They exited the building, keeping an extra eye on the nearby bushes and trees. All seemed quiet. Ben locked up, and they headed to the cars. Alyson's old dark orange Charger was parked next to Ben's yellow Mustang.

Ben turned to Felicity. "So, what's your ride of choice, another ride in the 'Sunshine', or you wanna join Allie in the 'General Lee'?"

Allie shook her head and gave Ben an exasperated sigh. "Give it up, Ben, I'm never gonna let you paint the '01.'"

"Come on, Allie, how can you have a dark orange '69 Charger and not make it the 'General Lee'?"

Felicity looked askance at Allie. "What is he talking about?"

Allie laughed and rolled her eyes. "'The Dukes Of Hazzard'. It's like a vintage car-guy thing. Anyway, you should let me drive you. You ride with Ben all the time."

Felicity could tell that Alyson must have figured out more than she had let on. She probably wanted a chance to talk to Felicity alone. The thought of trying to talk about Cain biting her made Felicity grow cold with fear.

She had thought she wanted to pump Allie for information about her bite from Sindy, but discussing the one she had received from Cain was out of the question. She just couldn't do it, not yet. She still didn't even know what to think about it herself. She deliberately took Ben's arm. "Sorry, Allie, I'm just a sucker for that smooth ride of his. Thanks anyway."

Ben smiled and then disengaged himself from her to open the door. Alyson squinted at her for a moment, as though she were trying to decipher something. Then she shook her head, got into her car with a wave, and left.

Felicity got into Ben's car. He got behind the wheel and stared at her. "What is going on?"

"What?"

"Is he scaring you?" Ben asked.

"Who?" Felicity asked innocently.

"Don't play dumb, you know exactly who I'm talking about. Did Cain hurt you?" Ben asked steadily.

She looked into his eyes, so he wouldn't worry. "No...no," she said quietly. It wasn't really a lie, but it felt like one. She knew what he meant, but she didn't want him to worry, so she looked into his eyes and lied. They were light brown, with little flecks of gold all through them. She felt terrible; she hoped he couldn't tell. After a moment, she let her eyes drop from his. "So, you dated Sindy, huh?"

He snorted derisively. "I saw her for a little while. Then we went to one stupid dance. I was fifteen."

"Did you kiss her?" Felicity asked.

He looked at her with shocked amusement that she should ask. "Yes. In fact, we made it all the way to third base, if you must know."

She tried to remember, "What's third base again? I forget."

He just laughed at her. "Ask Todd," he finally said. She rolled her eyes at him as he started the car and began the drive home. When they turned onto her block, she fully expected to see Sindy in the road, like last time. No one was to be seen. Ben parked in the lot. "Guess I'll see you at the dance."

"Yeah. Thanks for the ride. Goodnight."

"'Night."

He waited for her to get in before driving away. She suffered a brief flashback as she passed the pillar she had leaned against with Cain. Of course, she passed it every day, but it looked different in the moonlight. She shivered, ran up the stairs, and went inside.

Chapter 4 – Scorned

Cain

Cain's house
8:00, Saturday night

Tonight would be the night. Cain could not wait any longer; tonight, he would go to Felicity. Last night seemed to have stretched on forever. He had gone to great pains to avoid her, spending half the night holed up in his room. When he could stand that no longer, he had finally gone out.

It had been safely late enough into the evening that Felicity should be fast asleep in her room. He couldn't bring himself to go and check, but still, he made sure to go someplace she was almost certain not to attend. The next town over, there was a pub, just a dank little hole in the wall, really, but it was someplace to go, and he was sure that he wouldn't meet Felicity there. He had chosen a table where he could sit, inconspicuous and alone, observing people and trying not to think about his own concerns for a while.

About an hour before the bartender would inevitably call for last rounds, Cain saw Arif enter the establishment. He had three human women with him. Foreign beauties, their faces exotically painted and each wearing an ornate bindi jewel affixed to their forehead. Their bodies were heavily adorned with jewelry and scarves of silk bordered in gold thread.

They were quiet and demure, not even speaking to each other. Their only sounds were the musical clinking of their numerous bangle bracelets and the belled anklets that they wore above their slight sandals. Even these sounds would have been lost to the noise of the bar, without his acute vampire hearing.

The crowd parted for Arif and his consorts, as if by magic. He seemed to revel in the small stir that he caused among the patrons. He obviously regarded himself as visiting royalty, like some foreign prince or sheik.

He noticed Cain as he reached the back of the bar. He only momentarily paused in his stride, giving Cain a small smile and a respectful nod. Arif moved on towards a table of his own, settling himself into the back of a large, round booth, so that he could easily survey his surroundings.

The girls placed themselves around him and practically draped themselves over him as if to protect him from any other humans who might dare to approach. Cain had the impression that they would surely have put themselves on the floor at his feet if it had been possible.

Arif seemed to have had no desire to speak with him that evening, which was fine with Cain. He hadn't the stomach to place himself in the company of such distressingly bound slaves anyway; for slaves they surely were.

Of course, they appeared more than willing, but who could know what former circumstances had brought them to accept their present positions? Perhaps they enjoyed the protection, material wealth, and favor of their master. Maybe they had no choice, for surely a human with intimate knowledge of a coven such as Arif's would not be let freely back into society. To play the lovely escort to their master was preferable to being treated as a prisoner.

Most likely, they simply knew of no other life. Cain had tried to release such girls from their emotional bindings in times past. It was a most frustrating and fruitless endeavor. Their hopelessly scarred psyches were doubtless beyond his reach.

Cain had watched them for a moment as they coyly fawned over their master, and then he wasted no time in removing himself from their presence. He had given Arif a parting glance of acknowledgement and gone back out into the night until dawn had driven him home again.

He was glad to know that the man indeed bore him no ill will, not that night anyway. He couldn't know what the future would bring. Last night's excursion left his mind. For now, he could not look beyond this night. He would allow himself to go to Felicity at last. He took his time to shower, dress, and prepare, forcing himself not to rush.

It was Saturday evening, and Felicity was most likely working, as usual. He wanted to speak to her in private, without Ben hanging on their every word. He wouldn't arrive until almost closing time, just before ten. That way, he could enter before the doors were locked and convince her that he had no ill intentions and that they needed to speak alone.

Of course, Ben usually closed on the weekend also, and Felicity would feel that she could leave with him if she wanted, but perhaps it would be good for her to feel that security. Once she felt the choice was hers to make, he was confident that she would see the need for them to speak privately, if he could convince her of her safety.

He thought of waiting at the dorms instead, to remove Ben entirely from the equation. There was always the chance that she had told him, and he would be openly hostile. That was not a situation he wanted to deal with, especially not now, in front of her, but he rejected the idea with the unsettling thought that she might indeed leave work with Ben and not come home at all. That was an unacceptable chance to take.

It had to be at the DownTime; she would feel safe there. Besides, waiting at the dorms would remind her of what had transpired between them last, a memory he needed to keep held afar, at least until he could rein in her fear of him.

At last, he felt that he was ready. He had to take the motorcycle. To force upon himself the patience of walking would be just too much. He drove into town, and as he neared the bookstore, he felt her presence, still burning brightly strong in his mind. She was indeed working at the DownTime this evening, as he had presumed; he felt less affected by her mark, though. His body and blood recognized her and longed for her, to be sure, but he felt his rational mind was less influenced by it, and was sure he could speak to her without fear of losing control.

As he parked in the lot, he was heartened to see that Ben's vehicle was not even there. Could he be so fortunate as to escape having to deal with him? He hoped Felicity would still feel safe without Ben's presence. It was important that she feel Cain was not cornering her. He approached the door to find it already locked. He didn't wear a watch, but could see by the clock on the wall inside that it would only just reach ten in a minute or so.

He did not see Felicity inside, although he could feel her. There was an older woman and a young, well-dressed man, talking near the counter in the café. They hadn't noticed him. He would wait unobtrusively until Felicity appeared, and then knock. That way, it could be her decision whether or not to admit him. She would feel as though she were in control, and hopefully, unthreatened.

As he watched through the glass, Felicity emerged from the room behind the café counter. Cain was stunned. She looked absolutely exquisite. She wore a modest but truly enticing gown, and her hair had been elegantly swept up and back from her face. She seemed honestly to be the most beautiful vision he had ever beheld. She was also clearly planning to leave with the nicely dressed young man who now took her arm to lead her across the café to the door.

Cain had only a moment to comprehend this new turn of events before he was forced to rush back to the bike and leave the lot. However badly he would like to see her, it would not be like this. He quickly drove across the street and over into the lot at Tommy's. When he cut the engine, Felicity was still only just entering the young man's car. They had taken their time in exiting the building and locking the door. They hadn't noticed him.

Cain watched, dolefully, as they sped off past him, down the road. Who was it that she was with? He had never seen the man before, he was sure. She had seemed friendly, though not overly familiar with him. Cain hadn't been able to watch them long enough to really tell.

Where were they going? Should he follow? He decided against it. Why torture himself? He wouldn't follow after to try and ruin her evening or demand that she give herself over to him. That would be absurd. He would simply have to accept that she had interests other than him. It did not mean that she would deny him when he finally did approach, he hoped. He would simply have to wait.

He climbed off the motorcycle and entered the bar. It was as good a place to spend the evening as any, and he could definitely use a drink. He peered through the gloom at the various patrons. It seemed an older crowd tonight, not very many of the college students, who usually made up a large part of the customers. In fact, it wasn't crowded at all; odd for a Saturday night.

Alyson was also seemingly absent, a fact for which he was grateful. He sat on the stool at the very end of the bar, in the back against the far wall. Upon ordering a rum and Coke, he made sure that the bartender was generous with the rum and understood that his glass was never to remain empty. He left a nice pile of bills to ensure the man's cooperation.

Felicity's presence still flickered in the back of his mind. She was far enough that he could no longer feel her, but he could still see her mark easily. He kept waiting for it to recede, but she stayed stubbornly just within reach.

The college, Cain realized. There must be some formal school function that they had gone to. That was why the bar was so empty, and why Felicity had been so charmingly dressed. The college was too close; he would still be able to sense her. So even here, he would be tortured and unable to forget his evening's loss.

He downed his drink and considered leaving. Then the bartender set another glass before him and he decided to stay. What's the difference? At least he would know where she was and when she left. Perhaps he could approach her then. Before she has a chance to go somewhere else with the stranger she's with.

He knew he could not suffer to know that she was somewhere private with a man other than him. Not now, not after all of this. His anticipation and hopes for the evening brought to this bitter end. At least they were surely at a public function, surrounded by others. He quickly drank the contents of his new glass and tried to find something else to think about.

Unfortunately, the new topic that brought itself to his attention was not one he would have chosen on his own. Sindy approached. She was trying so hard to conceal herself, that he almost felt bad for her. Her trace in his mind blinked on and off like a Christmas tree light. She was making progress though. Eventually, she would learn the trick, and heaven help him when she did.

She was nearing the door. He decided to stand, to make himself ready for her arrival. He wasn't sure if she'd recognize his Harley out front.

Although he remained psychically concealed, he wasn't going to try to hide from her physically.

He felt emotionally fatigued and weary, and now that he had settled in, he was becoming comfortable here. He wouldn't let her chase him out. So, he stood against the wall next to his seat, with his third drink in his hand, and watched her saunter in.

She looked for all the world like a cat on the prowl. Every guy in the bar was intrigued by her presence, but she deigned to notice none of them. When she saw Cain in the back of the bar, she made ready to pounce.

He did nothing to inhibit her approach. They were supposedly under a truce, for all the authority Arif had anyway, which to Cain's mind was really none, but he felt Sindy would obey the man. She should have been told to leave him alone. So, he stood to meet her, trying to decide in his mind if her company was better than none.

He chugged the contents of his glass and put it down on the bar, as Sindy approached without the least bit of trepidation. "There you are, I've been searching. I wish you wouldn't cloak your mark all the time. I hate that you always make it so difficult," she said as she closed the expanse between them.

"You know what they say, 'a good man is hard to find'."

Instead of stopping at a respectful distance, she came right up to him, as though they were intimate friends. Personal space was a concept that she consistently ignored. "That's not what I say. I prefer the saying, 'a hard man is good to find'."

For emphasis, she reached down to rub his groin, at which point he grabbed her wrist. He kept her from touching him as she refused to take her hand away. He increased the pressure on the delicate bones there, but she still would not relent.

She was obviously in pain, but still fought him and forced herself to smile. Her voice betrayed her with a slight tremble. "What are you gonna do, break my wrist? Go ahead, at least I'll finally be giving you some sort of physical satisfaction."

At those words, he promptly let go, and she gave him a token caress there. "Come on, Cain. What's the matter? Are you so afraid of letting me make you happy in any way? I know you've got this whole 'passive aggressive' thing goin' on here, but maybe, deep inside your secret self, what you really need is a woman who can actually take what you have to dish out."

She lifted her face to his and whispered against his left cheek. "I know there is some major turmoil bubblin' just beneath the surface of that sweet, calm face you like to show the world. You need someone to rip into once in a while? You want to give some of that to me? Go ahead, I like it rough. I know some guys really get off on that kind of thing. Bring it on...if that's the only way I can get you to touch me. I'd take it... from you."

He held himself very still, unwilling to lose his composure. "That's not my style," he told her, his voice quiet but forceful.

She still persisted, whispering to him, her lips practically at his ear. "And what is your style, Cain? Innocent, doe-eyed little things that wither and die when you touch them? You can bring them nothing but heartache and death, no matter how you try."

He closed his eyes and tried not to let her words land in his heart, where he surely knew them to be true. She reached her hand up to the right side of his face as she placed a small, soft kiss upon his left cheek; the only tender and fragile gesture he had ever known her to make towards him. Her advances in the past had always been brash and bold, like when she had taken the liberty to touch him just before.

This was different; this gesture felt comforting and sincere, as though she knew his tortured heart and understood. He held himself as unmoving as a statue. Somewhere, in the back of his mind, he wondered if it wouldn't just be better to accept his lot. To accept the fact that Felicity, or any other woman, would only suffer at his hands, and here before him was one who could truly thrive in his hold upon her. Even as he knew it to be true, he refused to accept it.

When next she spoke, her voice quivered with such heartfelt despair that it startled him. "I can give you so much more than they ever could." Surely, there was hope for Sindy yet to change her ways. But right now, he needed someone sweet and tender; someone who could help him heal the loneliness he suffered from. Sindy could display that gentleness, but it was always fleeting and seldom heartfelt.

He wanted Felicity. He opened his eyes and looked at her with unconcealed heartbreak in his gaze. "You surely could." He saw undisguised hope and relief flash through her eyes for a brief moment, but he continued. "But I can't accept it. Not now."

Her eyes seemed to melt with sorrow before she brought back the malicious glint he so often saw reflected there. "Well, as a matter of fact, I wasn't here to seduce you anyway," she proclaimed, although she still held herself close to him. He hadn't the resolve to push her away. His words had pushed her far enough. "I was just here to congratulate you. You actually did it."

He realized with a guilty start what she was referring to, as she went on. "You marked her. I didn't really think you would, but I guess that just proves my point. You can act as civilized and aloof from me as you want, but we're really just the same, you and I. You drank her blood." She sucked in a slow stream of breath. "And I know you enjoyed it."

Sindy leaned close to whisper intimately into his ear once again. "Was it good? ...Did she cry?"

That broke him. He shoved her off of him with such force that she overturned the chair behind her. She righted herself and laughed at him, to cover any true feelings she might have. "You still wanna play with humans? I can play too. In fact, I'm gonna have me a good time! You can consider Benjamin mine."

"You're setting yourself up for severe disappointment. He'll never let you take him. Even if he did, no matter what you do to him, no matter what kind of mindless slave you might try to force him to become, the sad truth is, he will never love you. You cannot force someone to love you. You poor girl. What kind of past have you endured that you cannot see that?"

She had no words to rebuke him. He had never seen her eyes well with true tears in the way that they did now. He had touched the heart of her sorrow, of her anger.

Perhaps he shouldn't, but he pressed on. "There are other ways to gain approval from people. There are other ways to feel accepted and loved. Surely, your fine body is not the only asset that you possess.

Haven't you a fine mind at your disposal as well? Is there truly a heart within you, under all of the scar tissue and pain?"

His words seemed to strike her like blows. She flinched at each syllable until he thought she would finally break down and cry. She did not.

As his last words filled the air, she picked up his glass from the bar and threw it at his face. He jerked aside, and it smashed against the wall next to his head. As bits of glass showered him from the side, she turned and fled.

The bar had grown noticeably quiet, as its occupants became aware of their little drama. Cain was unsure how much they had actually heard, and found that he didn't really care. Let them think what they would.

He composed himself and realized that he must go after her. Not to redeem his words, or to confront her, but to ensure that she would not unleash her fury upon the next unlucky soul she met. He brushed the last shards of glass from his hair and followed her flickering presence out into the night.

Chapter 5 – Revelations

Felicity

The DownTime café and bookstore
Earlier Saturday evening

When Felicity arrived at work for her shift on Saturday, both Harold and Nadine were working in the café. She was in the bookstore with Lucy, who obviously felt bad, when she saw Felicity carry in her dress. Felicity hadn't asked for off. Lucy said she was sorry that she couldn't switch to close for her so that she could leave on time for the dance, but she had plans.

Felicity told her not to give it another thought. She did, however, apprehensively ask who she'd be closing with. She eyed Harold distastefully and thought about having to change in the lounge while he waited for her, probably trying to peek in the window.

It was with great relief that she heard Nadine would be the one closing. As the busy day wound to an end, Nadine called her over to the café. Felicity approached with a broad smile, grateful not to be stuck with Harold. "Hi, I was surprised to see you here. Don't you usually have the day shift?"

"Yes, I'm covering for Ben. He has that dance to go to. Don't you go to that school?" Nadine asked.

"Yeah, I'm going to the dance, just a little late. My date's picking me up here, actually," Felicity told her.

"Well, I can't pretend I didn't know. I saw your dress hanging up in the back. It's lovely," Nadine replied with a smile.

"Thanks." It was a pretty dress; she had worn it to her cousin's wedding. It was a long, champagne colored oriental style dress, sleeveless with a slit up one side. It also had buttons all up that side and a high collar, with a teardrop shaped cut out at the throat, just below the top button. It was demure, but very attractive in the way it hugged her curves.

Nadine folded her hands in front of her and looked at Felicity in the motherly way she usually affected with the younger employees. "You shouldn't be here so late; you should have told Mr. Penten that you had plans."

"That's alright, I don't mind. It isn't really all that important to me, it's just a dance," Felicity told her.

"And the boy?" Nadine asked.

"He's just a guy. It's not like he's my boyfriend or anything. We're okay going late," Felicity assured her.

"Well, all the same, why don't you go and close out your register now? You want to be sure and give yourself enough time to get ready."

Felicity looked over at the clock. "It's barely 9:30. I still have customers."

"That's alright. You just tell them to bring their selections over to the café when they're ready. I can ring them up here. It's not like I have anywhere to go."

Felicity smiled. "Thanks."

She was almost ready when she began to feel nervous chills travel over her. Her mind wandered to Cain and she felt a sudden wave of longing for him that astonished her. Not now! she thought to herself viciously.

She practically jumped when she heard the bell over the door. It was almost ten o'clock. She peeked out the lounge door to see who it was and let out a small sigh of relief. "That's him, his name's Todd," she told Nadine. "I'm almost ready. Oh, and you should tell him to lock the door behind him," she added, thinking of Sindy the night before.

She tried to shake that odd feeling that seemed to pursue her so often lately. It had grown quite strong, and her hands were shaking as she did the last of the buttons on her dress. What was wrong with her nerves? She shook her hands out into the air as if she could free herself through them of the jitters that had taken over her. She heard Nadine and Todd making small talk as she finished fixing her hair. She had put it up in a loose French twist with some curls falling down the side. It looked nice with the high neckline of the dress. She put her earrings on and hurried out to meet him.

He gave her quite a smile when she appeared. "Hi, you look beautiful."

"Thanks." She felt a little awkward, accepting the compliment. He was nice, but she really didn't feel anything special towards him. "Nadine was nice enough to give me extra time to fix my hair and stuff."

Nadine smiled and ushered her out from behind the counter. "That's alright, you two just get going. You're late enough."

Todd obediently took Felicity's arm and led her to the door, but she refused to leave before Nadine was ready. She wanted to see the woman safely into her car.

They waited as Nadine finished straightening up, grabbed her coat, and shut the lights.

Once the store was locked up, Todd opened the door to his car for Felicity. As she got in, she wondered if Sindy was going to show up as she had implied. She hoped that they could handle it without too much trouble. What if she said something inexplicable to Todd?

Her focus would probably be on Ben, though. She felt bad for him, as he'd most likely spend the whole evening looking over his shoulder, unable to enjoy himself. Undoubtedly, that was Sindy's intention all along. It would ruin Ben's evening whether she showed up or not. At least her own inner tremors seemed to be receding.

Todd looked very nice tonight, but there really was no spark between them. Maybe it was because things seemed too complicated right now, but she just couldn't see him as a prospective boyfriend. When they arrived, Todd parked the car, and as she began to open her door, he ran around to open it for her. Again, she felt a pang of regret. She hoped he didn't think this would be the start of something.

When they reached the entrance, they needed to purchase tickets, since neither of them had done it ahead of time. Felicity was quick to buy her own. Todd was a little surprised and told her he had planned to buy her one, but she insisted on paying for herself. "It's not really a date; we're just keeping each other company. I'll pay for myself." She hoped she didn't sound too harsh, but she didn't want to give him the wrong impression, and those were his words after all.

They entered the ballroom, and Felicity was amazed at how beautifully it was decorated. She didn't see Ben, but Karen and Jack found them almost immediately. "You guys look great! Let me get a picture!" Karen quickly whipped out her phone from her purse. Todd put his arm around her, and Felicity obediently posed, although she felt a bit awkward.

"Don't worry; I'll make sure you get copies," Karen said as she snapped their picture. They all stood and talked for a few minutes, and then Todd offered to go and get her a drink. When he and Jack left, Karen practically pounced on the opportunity to fire off a barrage of questions about Todd. "Isn't he nice? Do you like him? You look fabulous! He looks really good tonight, too, don't you think?"

"Karen, I don't want to disappoint anyone, but I don't think anything is going to happen between us. I'm just not looking for anyone right now. I hope Todd understands that it's not him." Karen quickly lost her smile, and Felicity felt like a heel. "I'm sorry; I know you wanted me to make him feel better. Maybe I shouldn't have even come."

Karen seemed disappointed, but shook her head. "No. I'm glad you came. Don't worry about it. Todd'll be okay. I mean, still give him a chance; you might change your mind, but don't feel like you have to force yourself to like him or something. If you both just needed to get out, then mission accomplished, right?"

"Yeah." Felicity smiled, grateful that Karen seemed to understand. The guys arrived with their drinks. "Thanks."

They stood and talked until Karen made Jack take her out onto the dance floor. "We'll stay here. I promised Felicity she wouldn't have to dance," Todd explained. Jack and Karen left with a laugh.

Just then, Felicity noticed Alyson across the room. Alyson saw her at the same time, but thankfully, she began to walk over, instead of screaming and yelling for her, as Felicity had half expected her to do.

She was wearing knee-high black leather boots with the black satin pants she had worn to Tommy's on Ladies' Night. She had paired them with a fitted, shiny pink satin blouse that was not buttoned at all until the very place where it tucked into her pants; being that Allie had such a slight figure, the shirt, although very daring, was at least not embarrassingly so. Felicity still had to stifle the urge to want to button it for her. She also seemed to have added some extra pink streaks to her heavily moussed and wildly shorn hair.

"Hi, I was wondering when you were gonna show up," Allie said as she arrived. She made no pretense as she obviously appraised Todd.

"Alyson, this is Todd. I didn't think you were coming."

"Somebody's got to watch the door for Ben; he's been a little preoccupied."

Felicity followed Allie's gaze to find Ben on the dance floor. He was wearing a really nice dress shirt of a dark golden color, with a black, gold, and olive-green tie, and black pants. The colors nicely complemented his honey-brown eyes and dark, wavy hair. He was clean-shaven and actually looked very dashing, but what really caught Felicity's eye was the woman he was dancing with.

Brenda was a stunning brunette. She was tall, voluptuous, and totally unlike someone that Felicity would have expected to take a class called 'Critical Issues in Law and Society'. Felicity would have to remind herself not to make such preconceived assumptions about people. She wore a classy, deep blue silk dress and looked extremely sexy in it. "Wow," she muttered.

"Tell me about it," Allie replied with a chuckle.

Todd seemed to figure out who they were looking at. "Is that your 'ex.'?"

"Oh...no! He's really not. He's just a friend of ours."

Allie smiled. "I don't think her 'ex.' is gonna show. He's not all that sociable."

Felicity gave her a warning look to get off the topic. "He's not my 'ex.'. He's not my anything." She turned back to Todd. "Maybe we should go try and dance, after all." She took his hand and practically pulled him to the dance floor to get away from Allie.

Once there, but not too close to Ben and Brenda, she stopped and looked at him. "You don't mind, do you?"

He laughed. "No, not at all."

They began to dance, hesitantly at first. Felicity had always been terribly self-conscious, trying to dance to fast songs, but she pretty much just copied everyone else, and Todd managed to make it kind of fun. After a song or two, she found that she was actually enjoying herself. She was glad she came.

At first, it was fine, but soon after they started, she began feeling flushed and getting chills, just as she had earlier and in the theater. When it began, she wondered if it might be because of Todd. He had been present each time it occurred, but…no. She studied him for a moment and knew almost instantly that it had nothing to do with Todd.

The feeling settled down into that strangely charged, pins-and-needles sensation. She felt it growing stronger and found it hard to even sway and dance. It was almost like a calling; a summons of some kind, as though there was somewhere else she desperately needed to go, although she couldn't say what had put that into her head. The thought frightened her. Mostly because the feeling also brought with it urges of a passionate nature, which seemed to wash over her every now and again.

The feelings were definitely not connected to Todd, but were beginning to make dancing so closely with him increasingly uncomfortable. She became overly conscious of him touching her, and the feeling was growing stronger by the minute. She began to feel inexplicably panic-stricken, as though she had to get away from the feeling, even as it called her towards it, though she couldn't say how or why. Maybe it was an anxiety attack of some kind.

Finally, she stopped dancing and looked up at Todd. "I'm sorry. This is nice, really, but I've gotta go. Please don't hate me," she pleaded.

Todd looked at her with confused concern. "I don't hate you, but what's wrong?"

She kept looking around as though she might see the source of her discontentment, but could find nothing to explain it. She wasn't sure how, but she was almost certain it had to do with Cain. She suddenly flinched and backed away from Todd. His hand had brushed down the side of her thigh as he took it off of her hip where it had rested, and it had sent a shiver through her. He looked very hurt and confused. "Nothing's wrong, I just...I need to go get some air."

"Well, let me take you."

"No, that's okay. I..."

Just then, Ben took notice of them and brought Brenda over for introductions. "Hi, you made it."

"Hi Ben. Um, this is Todd," Felicity offered, distractedly.

"Hey, how's it goin'?" Todd asked with a little wave.

"Hi, this is Brenda," Ben answered.

Brenda smiled and offered a "Hello".

Felicity was growing impatient; the odd feeling was as strong as it had been at the theater, and it wasn't going away. She didn't know what it meant, but it was very disconcerting. "Nice to meet you. I was actually just stepping out," she said with a little look of apology. She turned to go, but Ben touched her arm. It made her jump.

"Where are you going?" he asked.

"Nowhere, I'll be back," Felicity assured him.

As she walked away, she heard Ben ask, "Is she okay?"

Todd answered. "I couldn't really say."

After that, their conversation was lost as she made her way through the crowded dance floor. She thought she heard Ben call after her, but she kept walking. She thought she could sense the disquieting feeling beginning to fade as she crossed the room. It suddenly occurred to her that if the feeling was tied to Cain somehow, maybe it meant that he was here. She stopped and looked around again.

Ben caught up to her and gently spun her around. "Where are you going?"

"The bathroom," she lied.

"The bathrooms are over there," he said, pointing back in the direction they'd come. "Where are you really going? Are you okay?"

"I'm fine; I just wanted to get out for a minute."

"Why, what's wrong?" Ben asked.

Allie came jogging over to them. "There you are, I've been looking. Sindy's here."

Felicity looked at Allie in confusion. "Sindy is?"

"Were you expecting someone else?" A strange look of comprehension passed over Allie's face. "Oh. Is Cain here, too?"

She looked at Allie in agitation. "I haven't seen him." Alyson seemed to think that she hadn't answered the question, and was about to speak again when Felicity cut her off. "I've gotta go get some air."

Ben took her arm again. "Are you nuts? You can't go outside now!" He turned to Allie. "Where's Sindy?"

Allie looked around. "Well, she came in that door," she said with a gesture to the right, "but then I came to find you guys, and I guess I'm not as good at keeping track of her as I used to be," she added with a pointed look at Felicity, who wasn't really sure what she meant. She realized that Allie must know Cain had bitten her, but what did that have to do with Sindy?

Ben tried to take control of things. "Look, we're in the middle of a crowded dance floor. Nothing is going to happen to us here. We still have at least two hours left until the dance ends. We might as well try to enjoy ourselves, just keep your eyes open. We left Brenda and Todd just standing there. We really should get back to them. Just keep your cool, okay?" He looked closer at Felicity. "Alright?"

She answered him distractedly. "Yeah, okay."

"Come on." He started back to where they had left their dates. Alyson started to follow, when she noticed that Felicity had become very still and was staring unflinchingly across the room.

Cain, in the far entrance. He was just standing there, unthreatening, unmoving, just watching her. He wore a teal blue dress shirt, half buttoned, over his usual black t-shirt and tucked into a pair of black jeans. He scanned the crowd and then let his eyes fall back to Felicity. She was frozen, watching him. He seemed to be deciding if she would let him approach. After a few minutes, he slowly began to cross the room.

Felicity was panic-stricken and thrilled at the same time. She was frightened because she knew that the strange sensations she had been feeling were definitely coming from him, and she wasn't sure what that meant, but she also felt relieved to finally see him. Her heart pounded at the mere sight of him, and she was more drawn to him than ever, even though her mind tried to fight it. She felt caught between running to him and running away, so she just stood there, unable to move.

Alyson put a hand on her shoulder and spoke into her ear. "It's okay. You're in a room full of people; I'll be right over here." She felt Allie move away a bit and realized that Ben had gone on to Todd and Brenda, without noticing that she and Alyson weren't right behind him.

A room full of people; they might as well not even exist. She felt as though the noise was gone and the lights had dimmed. It seemed she and Cain were in their own private dimension, like she was seeing him with tunnel vision. He finally stopped just shy of her. She realized that he wanted her to walk the last few feet to him, to see if she would.

She looked at his face, his eyes. He looked just the way she always pictured him. Gentle, unintimidating, and handsome, with just a hint of a jaunty grin playing about his lips. He had such clear and honest eyes, the most beautiful shade of blue she'd ever seen.

She had to go to him. How could she not? She tried to remind herself of what he'd done, but then she thought of what he hadn't. He could easily have killed her. He still could, but she didn't really believe that would happen, and the longer she paused, the more his eyes began to fill with hurt and sadness. She went to him.

She stopped close enough to talk, without having to yell over the music, but didn't know what to say. He looked at her with a sad little smile. Then he looked aside, and she turned to see what he saw. Ben, with Allie, Brenda, and Todd, talking, unalarmed. Ben knew they were there and did look over once in a while, but seemed annoyed, more than overly concerned.

Cain looked back at her. "You didn't tell them," he confirmed with pleasant surprise. She opened her mouth to speak, but, unsure how to reply, she closed it again. He smiled at her, looking almost apologetic. "We need to talk, I know. This isn't exactly the setting I would have chosen," he said with a glance at the crowd of people dancing around them. "But I was following Sindy. I'll be needing to keep her out of trouble, I imagine."

Felicity found her voice and asked quietly, "She won't do anything here, will she?"

Cain glanced at her friends again. "You mean besides try to ruin Ben's evening? No, nothing too life-threatening anyway, but she can be unpredictable at times." He stopped to look into her eyes for a moment, seemingly judging her reaction to him.

She felt as though her skin was humming from his closeness. He hadn't touched her, though. She wondered what it would feel like if he did. She was glad when he spoke again, because she had no idea what to say. "Look, we haven't time yet for long, drawn-out explanations, which I can't really say I'm looking forward to giving." He suddenly looked around distractedly and backed away from her as if to leave. "I've got something to take care of, but I'll be back."

"When?" she asked indignantly. He was just going to show up like this and then leave, without resolving anything?

"Tonight, not long." He turned back to face her with a wink. "You'll know."

He circled around her, and as she turned to watch him leave, she was startled to find Allie standing right behind her. "Everything okay?"

She looked back to where Cain had gone, but couldn't see him through the people. "I don't know yet." She sighed and looked at Alyson in resignation. "You know, don't you?"

For a second, Allie looked as though she might like to make Felicity actually say it, but then spared her. "That Cain bit you? Yeah, I kind of figured that out."

"How did you know? And how did Sindy know? And if I can feel Cain like that, does that mean you can feel Sindy?"

Allie chuckled. "I don't mind playing twenty questions, but don't you think we ought to move it off the dance floor?"

Felicity looked around, suddenly aware of all the dancers, although of course they had been there all along. "Oh, right." She looked to find Ben, but saw only Brenda and Todd dancing together. "Where's Ben?"

Alyson put a hand on her shoulder. "Don't worry, he's talking to Cain. Come on." Alyson took her by the hand and led her through the people to an open doorway.

"I don't think we should leave."

"We're not." Alyson stuck her head out into the deserted hallway beyond the door. "Just trying to get a little privacy." She stepped out into the hall and settled herself against the wall just outside the doorway.

Felicity gave a worried glance around and then stepped out to face Allie. "How did you know?"

"Just perceptive, I guess. It's not like you hid it all that well." Felicity became alarmed. "Don't worry, Ben has no clue, but you know, you're not the first girl to ever be bitten for reasons other than hunger."

"Other reasons?"

"Guess Cain's explanations didn't get that far, huh? I'll let him give you the whys and wherefores, but don't try to tell me it was all bad," she said with a knowing smirk. Felicity was mortified that Alyson might know how she had felt when Cain bit her. She said nothing, and Alyson continued. "I'll just say that the times I've been bitten haven't all been accidents."

Felicity found that appalling. "By Sindy?" She was glad to see that Alyson found this revolting as well.

"Ew! No!" She considered a moment. "Not that I have a problem with girls in general, but it wouldn't be her! No, this was from Sindy," she said, gesturing to the scar on her throat. "I'm talking about these." Now she moved her shirt collar to bare the other side of her throat. Felicity couldn't even see anything at first. Then, as she looked closer, she began to recognize sets of tiny puncture marks, like she herself had received from Cain. They were healed and very faint, but they crisscrossed and overlapped so that she couldn't even tell how many times Allie had been bitten.

Felicity looked up in disbelief and then felt a wave of indignation pass over her. "Cain?"

Alyson looked insulted. "No, of course not. I hardly even know the guy." She glanced back into the ballroom to see if they were being overheard. There was no one nearby. She looked back at Felicity, and her voice took on a shy, quiet quality, which Felicity had never heard from Alyson before. "I see Mattie sometimes."

Felicity's mouth fell open in shock. "Ben's friend?"

"He's my friend too! I guess Ben's mentioned him, huh? Well, we've been more than friends, before and after, but Ben doesn't know that, and you can't tell him, ever."

"I wouldn't. Mattie's still around here? Ben thinks he's long gone."

Alyson shrugged. "He moves around a lot, but he always comes back to visit. He said I'd see him again before Halloween. I hope he's got the good sense to stay away until everything calms down, though." Allie looked genuinely worried about him.

Felicity didn't know what to say about Mattie, so she brought up more immediate matters. "Where do you think Sindy went? It doesn't make any sense, her being here. If she were going to do something tonight, then why'd she come warn us about it?"

"I don't think she came to warn us. No, I'll bet she didn't even expect Ben and I to be there last night. She came to see you."

"She said that, but why?"

"To see if you were marked."

"Marked? What is that, vampirese?" Felicity asked in annoyance.

"By Cain. Don't you get it? Cain bit you," Allie explained.

"So, what does that mean to anybody else?" Felicity asked.

"It means you are probably the safest person in this place. It's like having a 'get out of jail free' card." Felicity was staring at her in total incomprehension. Alyson started speaking with exaggerated slowness, as though she were talking to a child.

"Cain bit you. It puts a mark on you, like you belong to him now. No other vamp is gonna come anywhere near you; you're his," Allie assured her.

"Like the blood!" Felicity exclaimed in sudden understanding.

"Okay, now you've lost me. What blood?" Alyson asked.

"Cain gave me a necklace, a vial of his blood. He said others could smell it and they'd leave me alone," Felicity clarified.

"No way! Does that really work? I gotta get me one of those!"

Felicity just shook her head and laughed quietly to herself. Alyson looked at her questioningly. "Just something Cain said, when he gave it to me. He said it wasn't as good as the 'conventional method'. Now I know what he was talking about."

"I gotta be honest, I'd rather be bit than not." Felicity gave her an odd look. "For practical reasons. There are certain advantages. At least you only have to worry about one vampire getting you, instead of looking out for all of them. And it's not like they can sneak up on you," she said with a knowing smile.

Felicity recalled the feelings Cain's closeness had caused. "What is that?"

"I don't know how it works, but it's kind of cool, isn't it?"

"But wait, couldn't you use that to find Sindy?" Felicity questioned.

"Na. Doesn't last forever. It fades," Allie explained.

"Oh, how long?" Felicity asked.

"Three weeks, a month tops. It was kind of useful, but I'm not gonna let her bite me again, just so I can keep tabs on her." They stood in awkward silence for a minute as Felicity tried to assimilate this new information. Alyson got antsy. "Maybe we should go back inside. If Ben comes looking and can't find us, he's gonna freak."

"Yeah, okay." They moved back into the dance hall when Alyson stopped her just inside the doorway.

"Listen, don't tell Ben any more than you have to. He's very comfortable in the dark. If you put him on overload, I'll be the one dealin' with the fallout."

Felicity nodded. "Don't worry, I won't." She couldn't imagine Ben calmly listening to explanations of 'practical' vampire bites, anyway.

They re-entered the ballroom. It took only a moment for Ben to come and pounce on them. "There you are! I thought you were going to go stay with Todd and Brenda?"

Felicity looked at the couple in question; they certainly looked like a couple, too. They were dancing rather closely. She saw Brenda lean in to hear Todd whisper something to her. Then she gave, what looked to Felicity, to be a very well-practiced and flirtatious laugh. Felicity gestured for Ben to see them. "They don't seem to miss us much."

Ben was not pleased. "Great. Doesn't that bother you?"

Felicity tried not to smile at Ben's distress. "Not really."

"Thanks a lot."

"Well, what do you want me to do? Should I go over there and take him back, get him out of your way?"

Ben looked at her condescendingly. "He is not in my way. I could get her away from him if I wanted."

Both Allie and Felicity chuckled at that boast. "Is that so?"

"I could." He watched Brenda for a few more minutes. "Screw it. We didn't have all that much in common anyway."

Alyson put a hand on his shoulder. "You mean besides both of you being incredibly attractive? What else is there?"

"Very funny."

"Seriously, Ben. You set yourself up with these gorgeous supermodel types, then you get all pissed off when they're stunningly stupid and shallow, like you never saw it coming."

"The girls I date are not stupid and shallow!" Ben retorted, but no sooner were the words out of his mouth than circumstances seemed to conspire to prove him wrong. Who should approach, but Ashley, looking absolutely amazing and with a very handsome and athletic-looking hunk on her arm.

Felicity could have laughed at the way she most obviously conspired to guide her date into Ben's path and then affected that she hadn't noticed him until now. "Ben, hi! What a surprise to see you over here. I would have thought you'd be on the dance floor, with…Brenda, was it? Oh, wait, isn't that her over there? She seems to be having a very good time. I know I am. Enjoy the rest of your evening!" She gave a little wave to include Felicity and Alyson as well and then made her way out onto the dance floor with her date.

Ben watched her sullenly and then turned back to Allie and Felicity. "Okay, maybe Ashley fits the bill," he agreed grudgingly, "but Brenda's not stupid. And she's not all that shallow." He looked back over at the girl in question as Allie and Felicity smirked at him. "They're probably better off anyway," he said, turning to Felicity. "If Sindy saw us with them, they'd become targets for sure."

"Where is Sindy anyway? You don't think she left?"

"Cain said he was going to talk to her."

Allie looked steadily at Felicity. "Then we know he's keeping her safely far out of the way. Right?"

Felicity realized what she meant. Cain was definitely not in the building. "Yeah, right. So, you probably could go back to your date, if you wanted," she said to Ben.

Ben looked at Brenda again and then shrugged. "What for?" He turned back to Allie and then Felicity. "I've got two beautiful women right here. At least I don't have to worry about turning you two into vampire bait. You come with your own stakes and crosses."

Felicity raised an eyebrow. "Convenient."

Ben smiled. "So, what do we do now?"

"Let's dance," Alyson answered. Felicity gave them both a pained expression, which, in concert, they both ignored and dragged her to the dance floor.

After a song or two, Felicity thought she might actually be starting to like dancing after all. Karen discovered them and came over, presumably to make sure Felicity hadn't ditched her date. She pulled Felicity off to the side for a moment. "Where's Todd?"

Felicity gestured towards Todd and his newfound dance partner. "They seemed to hit it off, so I thought I'd stay out of the way," Felicity explained. Karen was immediately thrilled for him. She pulled her phone back out and made Felicity, Ben, and Allie pose for a few pictures before finding her way back to Jack.

Another slow dance began. Felicity looked to both Ben and Alyson. "You guys go ahead; I don't really like to dance all that much anyway."

She stepped back as if to leave, but Allie stopped her. "You're gonna have to take Ben, because I've got someone else in mind."

"Who?" Felicity asked.

"See that guy alone at the bar?" Allie asked.

Felicity saw who she meant, and he was definitely dance-worthy. "Nice."

"I thought so," Allie answered. "Do you know him?"

Ben and Felicity both shook their heads as Felicity asked, "So what are you going to do?"

"I'm gonna go dance with him," Allie answered.

"Just like that?" Felicity asked.

"Just like that," Allie confirmed.

Felicity smiled. "Good luck."

Alyson seemed undaunted. "Who needs luck?" she answered as she went off to claim her new dance partner.

Felicity faced Ben, hardly believing Allie's confidence. "Not exactly shy, is she?"

Ben gave her a look of disbelief. "Have you met Alyson? The girl's got pink hair and no buttons in her shirt. You thought she might be shy?"

Felicity laughed. "Well, good for her. I could never do that."

"Ask a guy to dance? Why not?"

She shrugged. "I'm just not good at that sort of thing."

Ben smiled at her. "A girl like you doesn't have to be good at that sort of thing."

"And what exactly am I like?"

"You know, different from Alyson," Ben told her.

"Could you be more vague?" Felicity asked with a laugh.

"I just meant that you're more like...my type," Ben clarified.

"Stunningly stupid and shallow?" she asked in mock outrage.

"No! I meant the gorgeous supermodel part," he clarified, sheepishly.

"Oh..."

"Hey, look, she got him to dance. Way to go, Allie!"

Felicity didn't even glance over; she was busy staring at Ben in bewilderment. "Did you just call me gorgeous?"

He looked back at her skeptically. "Do you own a mirror?" She was taken aback by his 'matter-of-fact' attitude. Before she could think of a reply, he continued. "So, are we just going to stand here?" he asked, looking at the dancers all around them.

"Oh, right." She hesitantly moved a little closer, and he put his arm around her waist. She felt awkward, like she wasn't sure what to do with her hands, but Ben seemed confident, and things fell into place. She looked up to find him gazing back at her with a smile. He really did look very handsome tonight. The color of his shirt brought out the golden brown of his eyes. They danced in comfortable silence for a moment, until someone next to them cleared his throat.

"Todd!"

"Hi, I'm sorry to interrupt..." Todd offered hesitantly.

Ben didn't say anything, but seemed annoyed as he dropped his arm from her waist. Felicity turned to address Todd. "I'm sorry we never came back. To tell you the truth, you and Brenda seemed to be hitting it off, so I thought you might rather I...kept my distance."

Todd smiled at her appreciatively. "Thanks. Would you mind if I drove her home?"

Felicity smiled, happy for him. "Not at all."

"Actually, I was asking Ben."

"Oh," she answered sheepishly.

She looked to see that Ben was much less happy, but seemed resigned. "I guess, if she wants you to."

"Well, when you didn't come back..." Todd began.

"I know. Should I go over and..." Ben started to ask.

"No," Felicity and Todd quickly answered in unison.

"I'm sure she understands," added Felicity, as Todd looked at her gratefully.

Ben gave Felicity a strange look and then turned back to Todd. "Okay. I guess you can tell her I said goodnight. I'll see her in class."

Todd nodded to them both. "Thanks, goodnight."

Felicity watched as he left them to rejoin Brenda, who was waiting not far off. Now she's gorgeous, Felicity thought. She looked at Ben, who seemed to have a hard time taking his eyes off Brenda. "Sorry. You didn't really like her all that much, did you?"

Ben gave a sharp bark of a laugh. "Have you seen her?" He gave Felicity a timid grin and sighed. "No, not really." He didn't sound very convincing.

The song was ending, but Alyson showed no signs of leaving her new prize. The D.J. announced that this would be the last song of the evening. It was another slow song. Felicity wondered if Ben would want to dance with her again, especially since they'd hardly even had a chance before Todd had come over, but he didn't even seem to consider it. The mood was broken. "I'm going to run to the bathroom before we leave," he said.

"Alone?"

"Did you want to come help?" he asked in amusement.

"I just meant, do you think it's safe?"

He smiled. "I know what you meant. I'm fine. I'll be right back."

As he walked away, she realized that she was feeling Cain's presence again. It was strange. Now that she knew what it meant, it wasn't nearly so disconcerting as before. Where before it had been odd and frightening, now she felt expectant and almost exhilarated. She turned to face the direction it seemed to be coming from. After a moment, he appeared in the doorway.

As he crossed the room, she found that she couldn't take her eyes from him. She was annoyed that he had disappeared before they'd had a chance to talk, but she was surprised to find that she wasn't mad at him. In fact, she had a hard time feeling anything other than an incredible attraction towards him. She wasn't even really upset anymore about the bite, although she felt she should be; she just wasn't. At least she was pretty sure he'd had a noble motive, and not that he was some out-of-control monster, which she'd had a hard time believing anyway.

He stopped just in front of her, but looked as though he wasn't sure how to begin. So, she did, "Last dance," she said simply.

He seemed grateful to be excused from having to explain anything just yet, but was oddly hesitant to dance with her. When he finally touched her, she realized why. It was electric. He took her hand and interlaced their fingers, and she felt as though no other part of her body mattered; like being in contact with him was the single most important thing to exist for. Her mind rationalized that it must be some kind of weird side effect left over from his bite, but...wow.

She wondered if he felt anything out of the ordinary. He put his other hand on her waist and pulled her in a bit. Her heart was racing, and she felt as though she couldn't get close enough to him. We are only dancing, stop being so ridiculous, she reprimanded herself mentally.

She purposely did not look at him. She was very annoyed at herself for letting him off the hook so easily and for being so incredibly attracted to him. What he had done to her should be considered inexcusable. Yet still, she found herself almost overwhelmed with desire for him.

Cain let go of her hand, and she rested it on his shoulder. He put his finger to her chin and tipped her head up to look at him, his slight touch upon her face giving her a renewed shiver of warmth and butterflies. "I know this doesn't excuse anything," he said, as though reading her mind. She sincerely hoped that he couldn't. "We'll still need to have that talk I've been dreading."

She tried very hard to ignore his fingertip, which trailed along her jawline, to fall off and move down the side of her throat. He took it away a split second before it reached the bite she'd received from him. She closed her eyes, forcing herself to think clearly. "I can't say I'm not curious to hear what you might have to say." When she opened her eyes again, he looked miserable. As though he was losing some inner battle. She couldn't have said what he might be fighting for or against if it wasn't about drinking from her...and she wasn't sure that it was. He gazed at her so tenderly, and his eyes seemed filled with such anguish, that she felt she needed to give him something else to think about. "Where's Sindy?"

He blanched, and she realized she must have picked the wrong subject. "Not here, and that's good enough for me." He shook his head and visibly forced himself not to continue his prior train of thought.

At least she seemed to have brought his mind away from whatever he'd been agonizing about. He smiled at her lovingly. She looked into his eyes and wanted to kiss him so badly. The moment seemed perfect, and she knew how amazing it would be. After what he had done the other night, she knew he wouldn't turn her away, but she didn't do it.

She refused to let herself commit anything to him until he was somewhat held accountable for his actions. How stupid would she be to want things to go further anyway? He was a vampire! She had never actually seen him that way, but if she hadn't really believed it before, she full well knew it now. So, they only danced. She knew her resolve wouldn't last forever, but at least she could feel somewhat in control for a little while. The song ended all too soon.

Cain sighed. "So, do you want to go somewhere else, or should I begin to beg for your forgiveness here?"

She smiled and looked away to see Allie and her new friend, deeply engaged in conversation at a table. "I don't know. Where do you want to go?"

She could tell that he was tempted to offer his place, but he must have realized that would be pushing things a bit. "Maybe we could just find a place here that's a little more private?"

She thought for a moment and then took his hand, trying her best to seem unaffected by the thrill of touching his skin to her own. "Come on." She led him out the doors and down a short hallway to the adjacent student lounge. As she held his hand, she was aware of a slight static kind of tingle there, but was growing able to ignore it, almost. The lounge was really just a small sitting area with a lot of big, comfy chairs and coffee tables. The overhead lamps were off, but there was a small lamp in the corner on, and the glow from the hall gave a little light. She chose a love seat, and he sat next to her.

It took him a long time to say anything. She tried to imagine how she would explain if she were in his position. She almost sympathized. He took a deep breath and began. "I want you to know that what happened..." He shook his head, as if those were the wrong words. "What I did was not simply for wanting to." She raised her eyebrows as if to question him. "I'm not saying that I didn't...want to, mind you. I'm sure you could tell that I did."

He paused for a moment, and she couldn't help but remember the soft moan that had escaped his lips as he had drunk from her that night. It gave her shivers. She hoped he didn't notice. He went on. "But wanting is something which I endure every night. It may be very difficult at times, but I do have control of myself. You must believe that."

She gave a little nod of acceptance. She did believe him. If he didn't have some control, she wouldn't be alive right now. "I did it because I was afraid for you. Afraid of what others might do, afraid that something far worse would happen if I didn't. I know that probably sounds as though I'm just rationalizing, and it must be difficult to understand."

She felt bad to make him struggle with words when she did understand the basic idea of the gesture. "I know about being marked. Allie told me. It's like the blood vial, right? Only more...undeniable."

"Exactly." He was obviously very relieved that she accepted that. "When Arif arrived and I realized that Sindy had allies, I was terribly worried for you. Sindy and her creations, I can handle in small numbers, but Arif is different. He is almost as old as I am and has mental abilities that I didn't understand."

That last sentence frightened her. "Well, where is Arif now?"

"I don't know, it doesn't matter. We've spoken, and I don't think he'd do anything to bother us. He seems happy to stay out of it. It's only Sindy that we need worry about, and she's nowhere near here now."

"What does she want with us anyway? Does she just enjoy trying to freak me out, or what?"

"Sindy? No, she doesn't want you at all. She won't even bother me anymore, I don't believe. Unfortunately, Ben is the one she's after now, but I've given him warning and weapons, I'm sure he'll be fine."

She had known this already, but it was still upsetting to hear it again from Cain. She was glad that Cain seemed fairly confident that Ben could take care of himself. She did realize, however, that he would come back from the bathroom to find her missing. She wasn't at all sure whether Allie had seen her leave the room with Cain. "Ben! I have to get back to him. He'll be worried." Cain seemed very disappointed. "I'm sure you've got more to say, but it'll have to wait."

Cain didn't protest. He stood and followed as she rose and returned to the ballroom. Felicity was very surprised to find that the dance hall was nearly deserted. A janitor was cleaning off tables, and a couple she didn't know were in the back. Where were Allie and Ben? Felicity turned to Cain, trying not to feel panicked. "Where would they have gone? Why didn't they wait for me?"

He shook his head non-committedly. "Haven't they their own cars?"

Felicity looked at him in confusion. "That doesn't matter; they wouldn't leave me here."

"They didn't bring you," Cain said matter-of-factly.

She turned to stare at him. "How would you know?" She became piqued and resentful. "Have you been watching me?"

"No! I mean, I saw you, but not like that! It's not as though I've been spying on you or something. You would know if I were."

She stopped and thought a moment, becoming more upset. "I did know! I've felt you. Not just here tonight, but earlier. And at the movies!"

Cain shook his head wearily. "That wasn't my fault. I was at the theater first. You came to me. If you think about it, you'll realize it's true. And I did see you earlier, but not to spy on you! I went to the bookstore to see you, to speak with you. I didn't know you had other plans. I arrived just before you left...and I didn't want to spoil your evening."

She pondered this for a moment and then accepted it. "Well, where are Ben and Allie? I'm sure they didn't just leave."

"Perhaps they only went somewhere to talk, as we did."

She barely acknowledged him; she took off for another doorway. "The bathroom." Cain followed along behind her. She only paused a moment before striding purposefully into the men's room. "Ben?" Empty.

Cain remained standing in the hallway. She came back out and stuck her head into the ladies' room quickly. "Allie?" She looked up and down the hallway. With the dance over, the building was quickly becoming deserted.

She turned to query Cain. "Sindy's not here?"

He shook his head. "Relax, we'll find them." He didn't seem nearly as concerned as she was. "They're probably just enjoying a rendezvous in a broom closet somewhere," he muttered as he followed her down the hall.

She turned to give him a dark look. "Not likely."

When they re-entered the ballroom, there was no one left. Even the janitor had gone somewhere else. Felicity crossed the room to the far exit, with Cain in tow. The double doors opened onto a sort of veranda, looking out onto the athletic field with winding stone steps down to the ground. As they left the building and went out onto the landing, Felicity scanned the parking lot. "Look, Ben's car." At first, she was very happy to see it, but then she became even more upset than before. If he hadn't left, then where was he?

"Is there supposed to be something going on in the field?"

She looked to follow Cain's gaze to the athletic field. The remains of the bonfire was there, with streamers and decorations on the bleachers, but that was long over. There was a small group of people out there, on the grass. They were too far off to be recognizable. They were just silhouettes, really, mostly obscured by a slight mist that was playing over the field. She felt herself grow cold with fear. She looked at Cain in desperation. "There are no other vampires around?"

He seemed unsure, but shook his head no. Felicity looked out onto the field again, in time to see someone get punched in the head and go down to their knees. "Ben!" she screamed. She took off and then tripped down the first three steps before stopping to take off her heels.

Cain caught her arm to steady her as she fought to take off the shoes. "Don't worry, she won't kill him."

Was that supposed to be reassuring? She gave him a fierce glare and wrenched herself free of him to run. Felicity practically flew down the rest of the staircase and then began sprinting across the field as fast as the slit in her long gown would let her. Cain was right by her side.

As they approached, she could see Sindy standing out in front of the rest, with her hands on her hips, waiting for them. Behind Sindy, she saw that it was indeed Ben who was down on his knees, backed by the largest, most muscular man she had ever seen outside of a strongman competition on television. Five others were standing around, Luke and Chris among them. Off to one side, there was another figure slumped, unmoving, on the ground. Allie.

As soon as she recognized Sindy, she slowed. He'd lied to her, he'd lied! He'd said there were no vampires near, and here they all were! Had he only been keeping her busy in the school while they'd done this to her friends? She turned to look at Cain, but he seemed in shock as well. She couldn't imagine what would happen next, but if Alyson had spoken truly, they wouldn't touch Felicity because of her mark. Only Cain could have her now. She had to get to Ben and Allie.

Ben was obviously conscious, but he wasn't even trying to get up. His hands were tied behind his back, and he had a large piece of tape across his mouth. Unthinking of anything else, she tried to run to him, but Sindy reached out as she passed and grabbed her. Sindy spun her around and threw her back into Cain, who was right behind her. She could have sworn that she heard Cain actually snarl. She fought to stand on her own, apart from him. Sindy smiled. "You'd better watch her, Cain. I can't bite her, but I'll bet I could still kill her if I really tried."

It was Felicity who spoke back. "What do you want?" She felt desperate to get to Ben, and she was afraid to see what they had done to Allie.

Sindy gave her a snort of contempt. "Like I'm dealing with you," she muttered sarcastically. "Cain's the one I've got a little proposition for," she announced with a smile.

Chapter 6 – Let's make a deal

Cain

The college athletic field
2:00, Sunday morning

Cain stood aghast and took in the situation with mute horror. When he had allowed Sindy to approach Ben, he had thought it would be alone, and he didn't think it would be tonight. He'd given Ben ample warning, and he had been fairly certain that the boy could adequately defend himself.

When Sindy did decide to approach Ben, Cain had fully expected him to chase her off. This was the last thing that he had anticipated. Cain had even been sure that he'd felt her leave. He'd had no idea she was here. He hadn't felt the presence of any others, and this was definitely not what he'd had in mind.

Felicity turned to face him accusingly. He realized things looked very bad for him right now, from her point of view. She must think that he had deceived her. How could he have been so stupid? He was the oldest among them, and he had been a naive fool.

"Arif!" He yelled into the mist as he realized the only explanation for the deception. There was a moment of silence, and then Arif did appear. He moved closer out of the fog from behind and to the side of Sindy and her men. Cain was furious. "Arif, do you so easily break your word?"

Arif spread his hands. "I have not raised a hand against you and yours, such was the extent of my oath. I merely have lent my psychic abilities towards the pursuit of my ward's endeavor. A pursuit which you so generously granted her yourself. I leave you to your own dealings now.

This does not concern me. I think that Sindy can take care of herself on this occasion."

Sindy stepped forward again as Arif let himself fade back into the fog and was gone. Cain felt the other vampires' trace lights seem to wink into existence in his mind as Arif left. Sindy addressed him in contempt. "Did you really think you were going to give me permission to try for him and I wouldn't get him in the end?" She was quick to pick up on Felicity's confused expression. "That's right. Cain gave Ben to me. A little present. I guess he cares for me a little more than he lets on."

Cain practically growled at her. "You know full well, it wasn't like that at all."

"You shouldn't make promises that you aren't prepared to keep, especially when you're playing with other people's lives. Maybe if you weren't so wrapped up in your own martyrdom, you could focus on other people's problems for a change."

"That advice doesn't carry much weight, coming from you."

"Oh, I'm sorry. I forgot. You like to be the one to give advice, be the teacher. What were you gonna teach me, Cain? Self-control? I'd say you're a little lacking in that area yourself lately, hmmm? Maybe Felicity could answer that for us. I can't believe you even got her to come near you again! I thought you'd be out of practice, but she's not even nervous around you! Very impressive!"

She came closer to question Felicity. "Did he come whispering promises of eternal life? Or...did you come back on your own, begging for more? Is he that good?"

Of course, Cain knew that Felicity hadn't really fought him when he had bitten her, but they hadn't spoken of it, and he was unsure just how much it had affected her. It was not the same for everyone. Now, Felicity turned away, and Cain could see that she felt degraded that others should know the experience had indeed pleased her. He was ashamed that she should feel so humiliated because of him.

He took a step forward, but without taking her eyes from Felicity, Sindy raised a hand to make a slight gesture into the air. The result of this was that Chris, who had been poised next to Marcus behind Ben, gave Ben a good kick in the back. It was only a warning, but it was unexpected and brought a muffled cry from Ben, which nearly drove Felicity to tears. Cain stood his ground and said nothing. He could see that Ben remained unbitten, although he'd certainly taken a beating.

Sindy dropped her hand back to her side and continued to speak to Felicity, as though uninterrupted. "It was real good, I can tell. In fact, I'll bet you loved it, as shameful as you think that is. It's not your fault, if that makes you feel any better."

In the following silence, Cain noticed Alyson beginning to stir. Felicity noticed too and was visibly relieved. Thank God, she was alive! She must have been knocked out and was coming to. She was tied, though, just as Ben was, and like Ben, she had a large piece of duct tape over her mouth. Cain thought that Sindy had seen Alyson's movements as well, but didn't seem to care. Felicity spoke to take Sindy's attention from Allie so that she wouldn't decide to knock her out again. "What are you talking about?"

"He didn't tell you, did he? Old as he is, he's gotta know. Some vampires don't, though. I was lucky, my sire taught me well, before Arif killed him. No hard feelings there, though, I kind of count that as a favor. The guy was a horror, but he taught me the tricks of the trade. He taught me about the venom."

She smiled as Felicity's eyes widened. "It's pretty nifty, really. It's a narcotic in the saliva. It's a vampire thing. Not just in the mouth, but actually injected with our fangs, too. Pretty cool, huh? It's supposed to ease the panic, calm the victim, make things a bit...easier."

She looked to Cain. "You don't mind if I play teacher some more, do you? It's kind of fun to have a captive audience, and I really would be doing a service to my boys." She turned back and blew a kiss towards Chris, Luke, and the rest. Most of them looked too stupid to understand what she was talking about anyway.

"It's a real rush, from what I remember, if you get bit by someone who knows how to do it right. If they drink right away, hardly any of it gets into the system; they suck it right back out. Then it's just enough to keep the victim calm. To be real good, they have to know enough to let the venom mix in first, get it runnin' through ya'. Then, it can be a real high, but like any drug, it doesn't work the same on everyone.

For some people, it doesn't do a damn thing. For most, it's just a nice buzz. Fuzz things up, slow their responses." She had been pacing as she spoke, but now she came to stand directly in front of Felicity again. "But I have heard - and stop me if this is just a rumor - I've heard that some people have a much more intense reaction. That it's something like an...aphrodisiac, almost. In fact, I've got a theory that it's a much more common reaction than people let on. Would you agree?

Guys tend to have that reaction to me even before I bite them. So, I can't say I've encountered real proof of it myself. Until recently, most people I've bitten weren't exactly up for an interview afterwards, if you know what I mean. But I have been experimenting lately, and I must say, it's been a lot of fun. I think Felicity knows what I'm talking about.

What d'ya say? Does it get you hot and ready? Is it better than sex?" She began to laugh at Felicity's obvious discomfort. "Look who I'm asking, little Miss Priss. Like you'd have a clue."

Cain had heard enough. "Lesson's over. Are you going to make us stand here all night? What the hell do you want?"

"You know what I want, but you're all convinced that you can't force love, remember? So, we're gonna play a little game. See, there's this saying I've heard. 'If you love someone, set them free.' Sounds like one of those boring morals you're always trying to instill in me. Except, I don't think you practice what you preach. So, here's another saying for you. 'An eye for an eye.' Isn't that Shakespeare?"

"That's from the Bible, you twit."

"Oh, right. You'd know, wouldn't you? Anyway, here's the deal. Go ahead and take Felicity, you want her so bad. You like her so much better than me, you think you can make her into a 'proper consort' for yourself? Fine, go ahead. Take her, love her. Set her free. Or...keep her, as a playmate, as a pet. Hell, you can even make her into one of us if you want. But know this, anything you do to her, I'm gonna do to Ben. Let's see how great your self-control really is.

In the meantime, I'll be your best student ever. Teacher's pet, if you can picture it, just as you asked. See, I know what you want from me, but why should I behave myself if you're not going to? I think it's a pretty fair deal. More than reasonable, really.

When you finally do get bored with her, or your conscience just won't let you keep her anymore, leave her. Set her free. I'll be here, living by your standards, and you'll have to admit that I've proven myself worthy of your full attention. If you decide to keep Felicity, then I'll keep Ben; everybody wins. There's just one problem. You went and got a head start. So, I get to catch up; it's only fair. Especially if I'm gonna have to live like you. Even the condemned get one last meal."

Even from here, Cain could see Ben's eyes widen as he realized what that meant. Cain moved to confront Sindy, but she began to raise that hand again. "Cain," she said warningly, "you know I won't kill him, but if you try to stop me, I'm thinkin' even you would be pretty hard pressed to live through it."

He knew she was right. Even without thought for himself, Ben, Felicity, and Alyson would die if he made a move. With Ben and Allie tied, it was he and Felicity against Sindy, Marcus, and five other vampires. It wouldn't be much of a fight. If he let Sindy do this, she would feel that she had won some ground. They would survive the night and figure out their next move tomorrow. He lowered his head to show he conceded.

Felicity saw him. "No!"

Sindy just laughed. Alyson sat up and looked as though she would struggle, but Luke crouched on the grass next to her, and she thought better of it. Sindy just smiled and turned to approach Ben. He was kneeling on the wet grass, with Marcus behind him. He stiffened as Sindy drew near. She knelt on the ground in front of him. He turned away from her.

"I know," she cooed. "I'm disappointed too. This is not how I pictured our first time. You're special, and although I don't really mind an audience, I would prefer to have you all to myself. But sometimes you just have to make allowances. It'll still be good, and if Cain can't control himself, the next time will be even better, I promise. This is just a little something to whet your appetite...and mine, until I can really take you, in private. Besides, this is just like your little fantasy. You and me, out here on the grass. Too bad sunrise is still three hours away, huh?"

Sindy ripped the tape off of his mouth with a quick, rough tug. Ben just stared at her, cold and silent. She tried to kiss him, but he held himself still and unresponsive. She leaned back to look at him, and Ben spoke for the first time so far. His voice was a little hoarse, but seemed almost eerily calm. "Don't bother with that. Just do it already and get it over with."

"Oh, Ben, aren't you gonna let me relive some of my favorite memories with you? I remember you being so fond of foreplay." She trailed her fingers along the neckline of her shirt, tugging it down a bit, enjoying the feel of her skin and the fact that Ben's eyes seemed hypnotically glued to her breast. "But don't worry, you won't need any. I'm really good."

She leaned into him again and began kissing his neck. Cain couldn't see her change, as she was facing Ben, but he could see Ben tense and all of the muscles down the other side of his neck go taut as Sindy sank her fangs into him. Alyson did struggle then and was given a hard shove to the ground for it. Felicity turned away; she wouldn't watch.

Ben closed his eyes, trying in vain not to react in any way, but Sindy was taking her time, enjoying her long-awaited feast. Finally, she pressed herself against him until he was forced to lie back on the ground. She lay on top of him, writhing in time to the rhythm of her suckling, trying to elicit some response from him.

Cain could imagine how difficult it would be not to succumb. Her hips pressed firmly against Ben's own, and Cain could hear the rumbling moans of pleasure that issued from deep within her as she fed. As much as it disgusted him, at the same time, he himself could not help but become aroused. He sincerely hoped it was solely the vampire nature within him that was responsible for his body's reaction.

It was going on far too long. "Sindy, don't kill him." He said the words strongly, but they sounded pitifully inadequate in his ears. Some protector he'd turned out to be. Sindy must have heard him, though, because she obeyed. She withdrew and covered the wound with little licks and kisses, as though she couldn't bring herself to leave the spot. Cain could see Sindy's trace in his mind, flowing forward into Ben, until he had his own, lesser glow. It had passed into him with the venom and would mark him until faded by time.

Sindy forced herself up from his neck, although she remained lying on top of him, her elbows poised, holding her up on his chest. She waited a moment for Ben to come around. "Was it good for you?" she asked in a husky whisper.

Somehow, he drew the energy to lean up a bit to look at her. He then spat directly into her face. She jerked back, caught by surprise, but then wiped it away and was unfazed. "Should I expect any other bodily fluids to come my way?" she asked with an amused smirk and a little thrust of her hips. He turned away from her with eyes closed, his mouth set in a hard line.

She practically slithered down his body as she rose from him and returned to Cain and Felicity. She shook herself in a little satisfied shiver and smiled. "Now we're even. Why don't you take your little girlfriend and go have some fun? Keep me apprised of any new developments, hmmm?"

She turned back around to speak to her boys. "You can leave him. I've made my point. He's mine now. No one's gonna keep me from him, if I've got a right to come back." She gave Cain a smug glance. "Arif said he'd see to that for me. Who knows, Ben might even decide to come back on his own. I can be kind of addictive."

She faced Ben; Cain wondered if he was even conscious. "Don't worry, lover, you'll know where to find me." She turned and walked towards Cain, pausing first next to Felicity. She leaned forward, and when Felicity looked at her, she licked her lips. "He's yummy." She moved on past Cain. "Let the games begin."

Her boys came to follow after her. As Chris and Luke passed by on either side of Felicity, Luke reached out and gave her cheek a caress. Felicity flinched away from his hand, and Cain felt an uncontrolled growl spring from his throat. Luke gave him wide clearance as he passed. Marcus came next, dutifully following after his mistress. Cain was happy to see that he had a large cross-shaped burn on the side of his face and numerous bruises and gashes. At least two of the other three that he did not know had also been stabbed, burned, and scratched. Good, at least Ben and Allie had put up a good fight.

Felicity stood frozen until they had all passed. Then, as though suddenly released from paralysis, she flew to Ben's side. He lay on the ground where Sindy had left him. Felicity knelt on the grass beside him and lightly touched his shoulder. He violently jerked himself away from her, presumably thinking it was Sindy again. "Ben, it's me," she said quietly. He stopped trying to arch away from her, but he still wouldn't look at her. She helped him sit up and began trying to untie his hands.

Cain made his way over to Allie. She didn't seem hurt at all and was miraculously unbitten. Sindy had far better control over her boys than he would have guessed. She must not want to give him extra reason to be angry with her, which was pretty funny, considering the extent to which she'd gone with Ben.

Cain began to try and untie Alyson's bonds, but she began to jerk around to face him and try to get his attention. Oh, the tape. He attempted to take it off her mouth slowly, but she was obviously impatient with that. In the end, he just had to rip it off un-gently, as Sindy had Ben's. "Finally," she said hoarsely. "In my boot." Cain looked at her questioningly. She just pushed her tied feet at him.

He heard Felicity tell Ben apologetically, "I can't get them," as she struggled with the knots tying his hands. He was slumped forward and didn't answer her. Cain wondered if he'd passed out.

Cain couldn't take the boot off because of the ropes that bound Allie's feet together. He slipped his hand down into the boot between her leg and the leather and then yanked it back out again with a sharp hiss as he burned his hand.

Alyson jerked her leg away in startled reaction. "Sorry, wrong boot," she said ruefully. "That's the cross. Try the other one." He looked at her in annoyance and tried the other leg. Eventually, he was able to reach his hand down into it far enough to find what Alyson wanted. It was a knife, a long, folded switchblade, held in a little pocket, which had been sewn inside the leg of the boot. He pulled it out and brought it up to cut the ropes.

Felicity had seen him retrieve the knife. "You had that the whole time?"

Alyson looked at her irritably. "I never even saw them coming. I got cracked on the back of the head and knocked out cold. What did you want me to do?"

Cain finished releasing Allie and walked over towards Ben. Alyson followed and held her hand out for the knife. Reluctantly, he gave it over to her, although he didn't like the impression that she didn't trust him to do it.

Ben was awake and aware of their approach, but said nothing. Alyson knelt next to him and tipped her head down to make him look at her. "You okay?"

"Great," he answered sarcastically.

Alyson began cutting Ben's ropes. Felicity was still kneeling on the other side of him. She obviously wanted to try and comfort him somehow, but was unsure what to do, and Ben wanted none of it. Cain gave them some space.

Once Ben's hands were untied, he brought them around to rub his wrists where the ropes had chafed. He was still sitting on his feet from kneeling. When he tried to maneuver himself to bring his feet around so Alyson could cut those ropes too, he clearly suffered a wave of dizziness. Cain stepped forward. "The effects from the..."

Ben looked up at him sharply. "Shut up." He then closed his eyes and held his head for a minute. Cain took a deep breath, for its calming effect rather than for need of oxygen. This was not at all what he had expected to happen.

Even if Sindy had managed to mark Ben, he hadn't thought it would be so blatantly sinister. He certainly hadn't thought that Felicity would witness it, but of course, Sindy had planned it that way. She had choreographed the whole scene to be as psychologically disturbing as possible. She wanted to be sure that Felicity would never willingly let him near her again.

Alyson cut the ropes binding his legs, and then she and Felicity helped Ben to his feet. It was no easy task and took some time. No doubt, his legs were asleep from being folded under him for so long. He accepted their assistance, grudgingly. Sindy had taken her time in feeding from him, and he was sure to have gotten a very full dose of the venom.

Cain wondered if Ben had been greatly affected by it, but was sure Ben would rather die than tell them. He seemed pretty clear-headed, considering, but his physical reactions were still a bit off. Ben stood for a moment and then shook their hands off of him. He obviously resented being considered incapable. Felicity turned to look over at Cain. "How could you let this happen?"

"I didn't even know they were here! Arif was mentally hiding them from me, I swear! You don't actually think that I would have agreed to this, do you?"

"And just what did you agree to?" Felicity asked him dangerously.

Cain shook his head and tried to think desperately of how he could redeem himself in her eyes. It didn't seem likely to be possible right now. He sighed with exasperation. "Nothing. I knew she would try, but...It wasn't supposed to be like this." He looked to Ben, who seemed to have regained his composure. "Ben, I did warn you. Tell her. You know I was trying to help. I had no idea those others were here; you have to believe me. I wouldn't have let this happen."

Ben only looked at him wearily and began walking slowly towards the parking lot. Alyson watched him for a minute and then faced Cain. "It's not your fault, but you can't expect him to be in a very understanding mood right now. He'll be alright. He's got me." Alyson turned to Felicity. "You coming?"

Ben had stopped a few paces away, waiting for them. Felicity was watching him. She looked as though she wanted to go and help him, but knew that he'd push her away. Not that he had a real reason to be angry with her. She turned as if to say something to Cain, and he could see in her face that she was feeling betrayed and unforgiving. It hurt him more than he would have thought. Cain spoke before she could. "Felicity, you have to stay and let me talk to you." She stared at him as though he were insane to think she'd stay. "Please."

"I can't, not right now."

He felt himself in a desperate panic; he couldn't leave it like this. "Felicity, please. I've less than two hours before sunrise. I can't bear to be imprisoned in that room alone, all day, knowing that you wouldn't even let me speak to you."

She seemed a little surprised at his mention of being shut up inside. Did she think he became unaware during the day? She seemed to waver.

Ben was watching her and then turned away in disgust that she might stay. "During the day, can you...? If I came to you..."

"Yes!" He pounced on her thread of an offer. "Please. Will you come?"

Ben began to walk away, Alyson followed, and Felicity was left standing there, undecided. "Maybe." She turned and ran to catch up with them before he could say anything else.

As he watched them leave, a seed of an idea began to form in his head. He would be shut up in his home all day. So would the others. He needed to prove to Felicity that he was not in allegiance with Sindy. Although he couldn't really imagine how that could be unclear. Perhaps he hadn't been as decisively against her as he should have been, but he didn't want to be considered her ally.

They were almost out of range, Sindy and her boys, but he could still sense them. He had never seen Arif's mark, but most likely, he was long gone. In fact, he was probably headed back to his harem and whatever sanctuary they used during the day.

Cain could follow Sindy and the others inconspicuously. He might have enough time to find where they slept before he needed to return to his own bedroom for the day. That was their only hope against these others, really, to confront them in the day. It would be dangerous, but he'd a feeling that Ben and Allie would be in a dangerous mood.

Cain didn't feel that he had a right to simply slaughter the others. Even if he could, that was never his way. They hadn't really done anything irrevocable, or even against him personally, but if Ben wanted revenge, he had the daylight on his side. If Cain gave their location to Ben, perhaps he, Allie, and most importantly, Felicity, would consider Cain redeemed. Then Ben could use the information as he wished; it would be out of Cain's hands. If Ben and Alyson wanted to go vampire hunting, how could Cain be held accountable? As long as he was able to follow the others to their hideaway unseen.

Cain hadn't any more time for conjecture. If he didn't move now, he would lose them. He surmised that dawn was about an hour and a half away. He hoped they would not travel too far from his own resting place. He had never sensed them from the house before, so he knew that they would be at least a mile away. He didn't want to get caught too far from home, but it would be worth it if he could regain Felicity's trust. He would manage.

Contrary to popular belief, vampires could move about during the day, when necessary, but it was very dangerous for them. If he were touched by direct sunlight, it would quickly burn and soon kill him.

Once he had been trapped by the day and had used a large umbrella to help get him home. It had seemed ridiculous and flimsy protection from death. Surely, anyone watching would have thought his timid progress and the oddness of his predicament hilarious. He'd thought himself doomed for sure, but he'd made it. He wouldn't care to try it again, but he knew it could be done. Likewise, if the day were very overcast, he could go out, but again, at great risk. Following in the shadows of unpredictable clouds was not his idea of a thrill.

He looked up to judge the sky. It did look like it would rain. Maybe luck was with him, better wet than dust. He hurried after the others.

Chapter 7 – Just visiting

Felicity

Sunday afternoon

When Felicity awoke, it was nearly two o'clock in the afternoon. She vaguely remembered someone banging on her door earlier about her mom being on the phone. She had told them she'd call back later.

Alyson had insisted on taking them all home. She wouldn't let Ben drive his own car; they took Allie's. She'd dropped Felicity off first, which didn't seem to matter at the time, but now Felicity realized that she had no idea where either of them lived.

They had never exchanged phone numbers either. She always saw them at school or at work. She had a vague idea of where Ben lived, but she couldn't even go look for his car in the driveway; they had left it in the lot at school. She couldn't stand the idea of waiting around until someone decided to try to contact her. There must be some way she could go and find them.

She threw on some clothes and rushed through a perfunctory call to her parents. Yes, the dance was nice, yes, she'd had fun, and no, she didn't think that she and the guy she'd gone with would be dating. See you next Sunday. Love ya', bye.

She made her way outside. It looked like it had been raining all morning; there were puddles everywhere. Now there was only a damp chill in the air and big fluffy clouds racing across the sky. She stopped at the cafeteria to grab something to eat. She ended up with a ham sandwich and ate it as she walked. Neither she nor Ben was scheduled to work today, but she had the idea that if she went to the DownTime, someone there could give her Ben's address or phone number.

She managed to get Ben's home number from Lucy. She politely fielded questions about the dance and went to call from the employee lounge. No answer. She tried again. After a dozen rings, she realized she would have to give up. She didn't know if Ben was ignoring her or just not home, but she needed a new plan.

Tommy's. She would head across the street and try to get in touch with Allie. She walked over to the bar to find the place locked and deserted. She should have realized. The sign on the door proclaimed that the bar opened at four. She was impatient to wait, but she didn't know what else to do. At least she only had about half an hour to kill.

She went back to the DownTime, to wait in the café. Unfortunately, Harold was working. She did her best to ignore him and sat at a table by the window. Finally, at about ten to four, she saw someone drive up to Tommy's and unlock the door. She wasted no time in getting over there.

There was an older guy behind the bar when she walked in. He looked very surprised to have such an early customer, and he didn't appear in a very friendly mood.

"Hi, I'm trying to get in touch with Alyson." She was met with a blank stare. "She's kinda short, pink hair, she works here. I was hoping maybe you could help me?"

"I know who she is. She's on at 8:00."

"Oh…yeah, but I really needed to talk to her now. I thought maybe I could get her phone number? Or an address?"

The guy was shaking his head at her. "I can't give that stuff out."

"Please? It's kind of important. Maybe you could call her for me, I'd really appreciate it."

Just as she thought he'd say no, the guy pulled a phone out from a shelf under the bar. He took out an address book, flipped to the right page, and dialed. "Allie? Hey, it's Tom. Yeah, I know, there's some girl here for you. Yep." He handed the phone over to Felicity, who gave him a grateful smile.

"Hi, it's Felicity. Okay, thanks." She handed him back the phone. "Thanks."

He looked at her oddly as he hung it up and put it back under the counter. "All set?"

"She's on her way."

"M-hmmm. You want something?" he asked, nodding towards the taps.

She smiled. "No thanks."

He went into the back, and she decided to go wait outside. It didn't take long. Alyson explained that she had taken Ben back to her place last night, and he was still there now. She said that he wasn't talking much, but he seemed okay.

Allie's place was an apartment converted from someone's detached double garage, behind a house not far from Tommy's. It was a cute little apartment. It was sparsely furnished with what was probably second-hand furniture and looked very 'lived in', but cozy.

Allie led her to the bedroom in the back. The room wasn't very large and was dominated by a queen-size bed. Ben lay on his side, facing away from them. His nice clothes from the dance were rumpled on the floor in the corner, and he was lying on top of the covers wearing a t-shirt and sweatpants. He looked up at them as they came to the doorway, but put his head back down without a word.

Allie turned back to Felicity. "I'm gonna go make him something to eat. You want anything?"

Felicity gave her head a little shake. Alyson went into the kitchen, and Felicity was left staring at Ben's back. She couldn't help but be reminded of the night he'd slept over and she'd climbed into his bed. He was lying just the same way. She walked over to the bed without a word. As lightly as she could, she got on the bed and lay down next to him. She folded her hands under her cheek and snuggled up against his back just as she had that night.

She just lay there for a few minutes in silence, until he finally looked up over his shoulder at her. She peeked up at him and smiled. "Hey." He sighed and then rolled over onto his back. She scooched aside to give him some room. He just lay there, staring up at the ceiling. She propped herself up on one elbow to look at him. "How ya' doin'?" she asked quietly.

He didn't take his eyes from the ceiling. After a moment, he said, matter-of-factly, "Seven."

She stared at him in confusion. "Did you not understand the question?"

"Seven times I have been asked that question today, in one form or another," he clarified.

"Oh."

"Alyson has been hovering over me ever since I woke up. I wish she'd give it a rest already." He finally glanced at her for a second before turning his eyes back to the ceiling. "What are you guys doing, changing shifts?"

"She's in the kitchen making you something to eat."

He rolled his eyes and sat up a little to yell to Allie in the next room. "And I'm still not hungry!" He lay back down with a thump and then winced in pain. He lay still for a few minutes, seemingly contemplating a crack in the plaster overhead, and then asked quietly, "Did you go see him?"

"No," she answered.

He thought about that for a minute. "He bit you," he said with contempt.

"Yeah," she quietly confirmed.

"You didn't tell me." He sounded hurt.

"No."

He turned to face her irritably. "Okay, that's the short version."

She lay back onto the pillows with a guilty sigh. "I'm sorry. I just... I didn't. I'm sorry. I lied to you."

After a moment, Ben spoke. "You didn't actually lie."

"Yes, I did. A lie of omission is still a lie, isn't it? Besides, you asked if he hurt me, and I said no."

He lay back again as well. "I get the feeling that it didn't actually hurt all that much." He sounded disgusted. "And no, I don't want to talk about it."

"I didn't ask," she replied. "Anyway, it's all over now. We can just put the whole thing behind us and move on."

Now he sat up on the bed in disbelief. "Were you even there last night? This is not over! This is *so* far from over! We're like...the prizes in some sort of depraved, obscene game of theirs! They're never going to leave us alone!"

She lay calmly, looking up at him. "I'm sure Cain will find a way to keep her away from us from now on. Nothing else is going to happen. Cain wouldn't let it."

"Oh, *Cain* wouldn't? Because he was real helpful in keeping things from getting out of control last night, right?"

Now she sat up to face him, indignantly. "What did you want him to do? It was him and me against Sindy and six other vampires! Not to mention *The Hulk!* Did you see the size of that guy?!"

He lay down again in a huff. "Yeah, I managed to get a real close look at him while he was *beating the crap out of me!*" As he was speaking, he pulled up his shirt to reveal his stomach and chest, which were absolutely covered in dreadful greenish purple bruises.

Felicity gasped in horror, and her hand hovered lightly over them as if she'd like to try and wipe them away. "Oh, Ben! Oh my God! Are you okay?"

He just looked at her wearily for a moment and then pulled back down his shirt. "Eight. And yes, I'll live. I can't say I've been beaten worse, but at least I don't think they broke anything."

"Are you sure? What if you've got cracked ribs or something? Maybe you should go to the hospital, just to make sure you're alright." She interrupted him just as he looked like he might say something. "And don't you dare start counting at me again."

Just then, Alyson arrived carrying a little tray. "Here you go. Scrambled eggs, soft but not runny, with little bits of cheese in them; just the way you like 'em. Oh, and O.J., of course."

Ben gave her an exasperated sigh. "Alyson, I do not want eggs."

She looked down at the tray, as though wondering what was wrong with them. "Well, what do you want?"

He stared at her for a minute and then propped himself up on his elbows. "I *want* to wake up next to Brenda, to find that this was all some awful nightmare, but I guess *that's* not going to happen, huh?"

Alyson stood there staring at the eggs. After a moment, Felicity inquired disapprovingly, "You'd sleep with her on the first date?"

Ben glared at her for a second. "Thank you, Felicity, for putting this in perspective, because my *morals* are the real issue right now!" he replied sarcastically. She shook her head and looked away.

"You have to eat something," Allie demanded. She took the orange juice off the tray and tried to hand it to Ben, who wouldn't accept it. "Just take it and drink it already! You lost a lot of blood, and you need to rebuild your strength."

As she finally managed to shove the glass into his hand, Ben muttered angrily, "You're the expert." As Ben took a sip, Allie looked over at Felicity questioningly. She shook her head and gave a little shrug to show that she didn't know what he meant.

Alyson questioned him. "Are you mad at me?" she asked, putting the tray down on her dresser.

He looked up from the glass. "Why should I be mad at you?" he asked with another twinge of sarcasm.

"I don't know, but you've been giving me the angry vibe all day. What'd *I* do?"

Ben sat up a little more, beginning to look angry. "Four times."

Felicity shook her head in annoyance. "What is with the new number fetish?"

Ben paid her no attention and continued. "Wasn't it four times at last count?" Allie just shrugged. "You have been bitten four times and you never told me!"

"Told you what?"

"That it was like a drug!" Ben demanded.

"What for?" Alyson inquired with indifference.

Ben became infuriated. "I don't know, as an interesting sidebar? A footnote? My best friend's been bitten four times in three years, and I had no clue it was intoxicating! You'd think I would've heard about something like that!"

Alyson spoke calmly and quietly in contrast with Ben's yelling. "What would've been the point?"

"I just...I didn't expect it to be like *that*. I didn't know."

"Well, now you know," Allie said quietly.

"Now I know." He stared at her in resentment for a few minutes before asking, "Do you have any money?"

She seemed taken aback by the abrupt shift in topic, but dug into her back pocket. "I think I've got a twenty."

"No, in the bank," he clarified.

"About two months' rent. Why?" Allie asked.

He didn't answer her, but turned to Felicity. "How about you?"

Felicity spread her hands. "I'm lucky if I've got fifty bucks."

He seemed to be figuring something out in his head. "I haven't got much, since I spent it all on the 'stang, but I've got some. It'll have to do. We're going on vacation."

Alyson laughed. "What?"

"I'm thinking Vermont," Ben informed them.

Felicity stared at him as if he'd lost his mind. "Are you lightheaded? How much blood did you lose?"

He turned to her earnestly. "Allie's told me all about the 'mark' thing. And about the tracking...location vibe. I don't want to feel it. I don't want them to know where we are. I just want us far away from here, the three of us." He turned back to Allie. "How long does it take? Three weeks?"

She shook her head apologetically. "She dosed you up pretty good." He flinched a little at her words. "I'm thinkin' more like four."

"Okay, a month then. And when it's gone, we'll be free. We can go anywhere that we want; they'll never find us. Felicity can go back to her folks if she wants," he said, turning to Felicity. "They don't know where you live. Allie and I...we'll just have to find someplace else. Or, if it seems feasible, we could come back," he paused to give a meaningful look to Alyson, "and kill them all." Felicity couldn't tell what Allie thought of that. She was just staring at him silently. "But we should stick together at first. Let's go to Vermont."

Felicity took his hands from his lap as she sat next to him on the bed. "Ben, I understand how you must feel, but I'm not going to Vermont."

"Come on," he said with a persuasive little smile. "You'd make a great ski bunny. Besides, at least you're only dealing with Cain. I can't speak for his motives, but at least he's not a lunatic. Look at who I've got to deal with! Have you seen what she does to those guys? I've got higher goals in life than 'zombie love-slave', I've gotta tell ya."

Alyson spoke quietly from behind him. "I can't leave."

He turned to face her, dropping Felicity's hands. "Why not? It's not like you have anyone here but me anyway."

"I know, but I don't wanna leave. Besides, they don't even want me," Allie insisted.

"Yes, but if we disappear, who do you think they'll take it out on?" Ben asked.

"I can't leave right now, at least not until after Halloween." Felicity's eyes grew wide as she stared at Alyson over Ben's head. She tried desperately to make her understand that it was a really bad idea to do this now. Allie absently walked around the bed and went to stand in front of the closet door, playing with her fingernails.

Ben was perplexed. "It has to be now, that's kind of the point. We've got big bull's eyes painted on us for the next month. What's on Halloween?"

Allie tried to act nonchalant, but wasn't really pulling it off. "Nothing. I just told someone I'd be around, and I don't want to blow him off."

Ben stood up from the bed and turned to face her. "Are you kidding? You're going to get killed over some guy?" Allie just looked away. "Who is he? That guy from the dance?"

"No, I think Sindy and her thugs probably scared the shit out of him. I'll have to remember to thank her for that."

"Then who? You can't be all that serious if I don't even know him," Ben insisted.

Felicity gave Allie a desperate look that went totally unheeded. She knew what was coming, but seemed powerless to prevent it. Alyson spoke quietly. "You don't want to know."

"Like that answer doesn't just make it ten times worse. Gimme a name. What is he, a friend of mine?" She gave the slightest nod. "Is it Jeff, Pete, who?"

"Yeah, like any of your yuppie college buddies would ever look twice at me."

"Then who?"

Alyson refused to answer but finally looked up to meet his eyes, pleading silently for him to understand. Ben stared at her uncomprehending. Alyson's hand seemed to rise of its own accord to touch her fingers to the nearly invisible bite marks on her neck. Felicity wasn't even sure if it was a conscious gesture, but it did serve to give Ben a nudge of understanding.

In the growing silence, he suddenly went very pale. He started shaking his head in disbelief and seemed to mouth the word 'no' a few times, silently. Then he stopped to stare stonily at Alyson. "Say it. I dare you to say it."

She seemed to become aware of her hands again and clutched them nervously in front of her. She stared at her finely manicured fingernails as if they were foreign objects. Finally, she whispered, "It's Mattie."

Ben flew into a rage. "It is *not* Mattie! It's a blood sucking demon walking around in my best friend's skin!"

Alyson jerked her head up to look him in the eye. "It *is* Mattie, Ben. I know it is. We've spent time together; we've talked about stuff. I know him!"

"Not as well as I did."

"Better than you do! Even before he died."

Ben's face managed to grow even paler than before. "It's not really him."

"Yes, it is Ben. He's just the same. Trust me."

"Trust you? You've been hiding this from me for three years! Longer if you count anything that happened before they got him! If you're so convinced that he's okay, then why'd you hide it from me?"

Another wave of comprehension passed over his face, and Ben went from looking resentful to shocked and then even more enraged than before. He spoke in a quiet voice that was so smoldering with anger that it frightened Felicity, and it wasn't even directed at her. "Is it still four? Is it? Or were those only the ones you couldn't hide? What's the magic number, Allie? What else have you been keeping from me?"

Before Alyson could even answer, he crossed the room, grabbed the collar of her shirt, and ripped it away from her neck. She tried to protest, but he shoved her up against the closet door and pushed her head to the side so that he could have a clear view of her throat. He stared in silence and then thrust her head to the other side. She just stood there and let him look.

He clenched his hands into tight fists for a moment and then opened his hand to slam his right palm against the closet door next to her head with a loud bang. "Damn it, Allie! You blood whore!" he yelled at her in disgusted disbelief. He pushed himself off the wall away from her and stormed out of the room.

Allie just stood there for a moment with her eyes closed, hearing him stomp around her apartment. She opened her eyes to look at Felicity on the bed. "And that's why I didn't tell him." She ran a hand through her hair and was startled when he bounded back into the room.

"Where are my shoes?"

"Ben, don't go."

"Where are my God damned shoes?"

Allie seemed shaken and quickly stood away from the wall. "Don't go, I'll go. I'm gonna go out for a while. Stay here, please. I'm gonna go over to Tommy's and tell them I'm not coming in tonight. I've got some stuff to do. I'll be back in a little while. You just stay here and chill, okay?" Alyson gave him no time to answer and quickly left. Felicity supposed that Alyson was afraid that if she let Ben leave, he might never come back.

He sat on the bed with his head in his hands, facing away from her. Felicity watched him for a minute. Then she moved closer and tried to lightly put a hand on his shoulder. "She really cares about him, you know."

He jerked away from her touch so violently that it scared her. He turned to face her. "What do you know? Get out." He put his head back into his hands. She got up off the bed, but couldn't bring herself to leave him so upset. She just stood there, biting her tongue and fighting back tears. Ben spun around angrily to see why she hadn't left. He must have realized that he was frightening her, because he abruptly toned it down, but he was still firm. "I'm sorry. I just want to be alone right now."

She didn't say another word; she just turned and left. When she got outside, she saw that Allie was just sitting in her car. Felicity bent to knock lightly on the window. Alyson looked up, startled. She was crying. Felicity went around to the passenger door and got in. She looked at Allie, who was wiping her face. "He'll get over it," Felicity offered. "He's just...on overload."

"I know. He can't stay mad at me. He's like my only family, by choice, but still. Ever since his mom died, we take care of each other, you know?" Felicity gave her a tender smile. Alyson sniffled and grabbed a tissue out of the glove compartment to finish wiping her face.

"I keep thinking some girl is gonna come along and finally take him off my hands, but you know Ben, he's never satisfied." She shrugged. "He needs me. Otherwise, I probably wouldn't even be here right now." Felicity looked at her questioningly. "Mattie's offered you know." She nodded towards the apartment. "You think this was bad, Ben would have a total conniption if I told him that. Mattie wants me to come with him, to be like him."

Felicity tried to keep her face carefully neutral. "What did you tell him?"

Alyson smiled. "To ask me again in ten years, before I start gettin' old." She laughed at Felicity's expression of wonder tinged with fright. "Scary stuff."

"Death?"

"Life. All of it. I don't know. I'm not going anywhere right now, though, I can tell you that." She pulled herself together, threw the wad of tissues into the backseat, and started the car. "I've got some stuff to do. Let him cool off for a while. I'm glad we never went and got his car; he'll stay. You need a ride somewhere?"

Felicity thought about it as she stared at the car's digital clock. Its little green glowing numbers read 6:09 p.m. It would be getting dark in about an hour, not much time. "You guys are going to stay holed up at your place tonight?"

"Unless I come home to find out Ben's booked us a trip to Vermont. Come back later if you want. Here..." She found a scrap of paper and scribbled down her phone number and address. "Call if you need me to come pick you up."

She smiled. "Thanks. Can you drop me at the cemetery?"

Alyson's eyes widened. "Yeah, sure." She pulled out and started down the road. "Gonna go see him, huh?"

"What else is there to do?"

"He doesn't really live in the cemetery, does he?"

"No, just makes for a shorter walk. I don't think it'd be fair for me to..."

"Yeah, that's cool. A vamp's resting place is kind of private. I get that. He must really trust you."

"I guess. Hey, do you want me to ask him anything?"

"Like what?"

"Well, I don't know for sure, he didn't say anything, but... He was there when Ben told me about Mattie. I got the feeling that Cain knows him."

Alyson perked up immediately. "You think?"

She shrugged. "I could ask."

"Just tell him I'm worried."

"I will."

Alyson dropped her off at the cemetery, and she walked the rest of the way to Cain's. She wasn't really frightened of him, but she was glad that it was still daylight. She'd thought about things and decided that Cain was telling the truth. He hadn't known what Sindy had planned; he wouldn't have let that happen. If he had expected her to do something like that, he would have been better prepared. Maybe he should have anticipated it, but it wasn't intentional.

She couldn't stop hearing the heartbreak in his voice when he'd asked her to stay and talk last night. It had seemed so important to him that she not reject him. Did he care for her that much? Was he so desperate to be close with her? She felt that way, too, but she kept telling herself how irrational it was, how it would be insane to let him draw her that close to him. Yet, here she was.

She could feel him. As she turned up the driveway, it grew even stronger. She stopped to analyze it for a moment, now that she recognized what it was. It was like the direction in which he lay beckoned her, tried to draw her closer to him. Her body tingled with anticipation.

She thought about Sindy and the others, how they attacked people unaware and then left them. Those people would be walking around the next day feeling this? What would they make of it, how much would they remember? Would they think they were ill? Some might even find it curiously exciting and get close enough to let themselves get bitten again, before they understood.

She had memories of a lovely movie maiden, two perfect dots of a puncture wound, dark against her pale throat. Dressed in a beautiful gossamer nightgown, she would awaken in the night to go out and meet her vampire lover. Felicity had always thought the maiden was so stupid to let herself be put into such a trance. And yet, here she was. She'd changed from her gown into jeans and a peasant blouse, but she went to him all the same.

At least it was daylight, she thought with self-assurance. At the instant the thought came to her mind, a large cloud blotted out the sun, placing her in dark shadow. She looked up at the sky, as if she were the butt of some cosmic joke. "That's not funny."

She hung her head in resignation and climbed the steps to the front door. She hesitated for a moment, wondering if he would even hear her knock from down in the basement. He did have very keen hearing, but he was probably sleeping. That made her wonder again, whether it was like normal sleep. She raised her hand to knock, when the door opened from within, startling her.

Cain stood in the shadow of the doorway seeming very relieved to see her. Felicity was struck anew at how handsome he was. She felt as though she was buzzing with excitement at the sight of him. She stood frozen for a second and then dropped her hand back down to her side. "And I was afraid that you wouldn't hear me knock."

He gave her a roguish smile. "I felt you coming from nearly a mile away."

She was a little embarrassed to hear him speak so openly of the amazing bond they now shared. It made her wonder if it was different for him, or if he felt it in just the same way. "I thought you would be sleeping."

"You woke me up." Somehow, he managed to make even that innocuous sentence sound suggestive.

"Sorry." She knew she must be blushing and tried not to meet his gaze. She felt foolish for being so affected by him. He simply stood there, inside the doorway, drinking her in with his eyes. When she did look up at him, she realized something was different. She couldn't put her finger on it. It was most subtle, but he did seem changed somehow. Her curiosity overcame her shyness. "You look...different."

He became self-conscious, and she felt terribly rude. "It's nothing. Just a little sunburn."

It took her a second to realize the peculiarity of that statement. "What did you do?"

He smiled sheepishly. "Forgot my umbrella." Just then, the sun poked out from behind a cloud and bathed the porch in sunlight. Cain was protected where he stood, but he still flinched. "Can we talk downstairs?" She didn't answer immediately, and he became a little offended. "I wouldn't..." He stopped himself and sighed. "Or we could sit here on the floor by the door, if you'd like."

She felt ridiculous. "No, of course we can go downstairs." He backed away from the door to let her in and then quickly closed it behind her. She couldn't imagine what it would be like to have something so fatal all around you. She thought it might be rather terrifying. No wonder they slept all day. She began to follow him downstairs. "So, you can be awake during the day, if you want?" Obviously, it was true, but it still seemed strange.

"You can be awake during the night, can't you?"

"Yeah, but I always thought vampires were like, comatose until nightfall," she said in defense.

"Would those be the same vampires that prefer to sleep in coffins?" he asked in amusement.

"Yeah, that'd be them," she replied sheepishly.

"I can't say *I* slept much at all, really. I thought perhaps I'd see you sooner."

They entered the basement and crossed the room to sit on the bed. "I was busy," she said with an annoyed tone. She hadn't meant for it to come out so cold, but she wanted to make it clear that she was not so bound to him, that she should put him before all else.

He seemed to get the point. "With Ben, of course. Is he alright?"

"Nothing that time and a whole lot of therapy can't cure."

Cain sat next to her on the bed and looked down into his lap, chastened. "Do you believe me when I tell you that it was beyond my knowledge or control?"

"If I didn't, I wouldn't be here," she said firmly.

He nodded his head once in acceptance. "So, what is Ben planning?"

His business-like attitude threw her off. "Planning?"

"I don't suppose he's just going to wait around to see if she'd like some more. No matter what fool game Sindy thinks she's playing, I know her. Benjamin holds some special significance for her, perhaps because she knew him in life. She sees him as a conquest. I'd like to say that she should be satisfied, having proven herself master to him now. Perhaps she even will attempt to live as I do and leave him alone; I do hope she'll try, but more likely, now that she's had a taste of him, she won't ever quite be able to let him be."

Felicity felt prompted to ask him just *how* he lived. Sindy had insinuated that he didn't usually drink from people, but Felicity was still unsure. It seemed something that she ought to get clear, but Cain continued speaking before she had a chance to ask.

"Also, knowing Benjamin as I do, I don't think he'll give her a second chance. Thoughts of revenge must be running through him even as we speak. I know I've had similar thoughts of my own. So, what is he planning?"

Felicity fidgeted a bit on the bed, losing her train of thought. Her own body seemed quite powerfully aware of Cain's physical presence. The urge to touch him, in any way, was so strong that it was distracting. She fought to ignore it and answer his question. "Right now, the only thing I'm aware that he's planning is a vacation. He wants us to leave; me, him, and Allie, for at least a month, maybe longer."

"Until the mark fades. Ben is a smarter man than I give him credit for. Not that I ever doubted his intelligence, but it can be a difficult thing to let your actions be led by your mind and not your emotions. I have a little trouble with that myself sometimes." He looked very thoughtful and a little sad. "When are you leaving?"

"I don't know. Do you think we need to?"

He looked at her for a long time before answering; she began to wonder if he was going to. "I'd like to say no, but I'm having trouble sorting whether that'd be my mind or my emotions." He fidgeted a bit on the bed and looked away from her, down at the floor. "To be perfectly honest, I'd had that same plan for you myself. Only in my head, I was going with you. Active imagination, I've got, eh?"

That brought to mind frightening things that Sindy had said the night before, about Cain wanting to keep Felicity as a 'consort' or maybe a 'pet'. Of course, Sindy had chosen her words carefully; the whole thing had been designed to spook her. To a certain extent, it had worked. She was uncertain how much to believe. She'd be a fool to discount all of it as scare tactics, as much as she'd like to.

As he was looking away, she found herself staring at him, at the side of his face. He had only a hint more color in his cheeks now and across his nose. It wouldn't be noticeable to anyone else, really. She wouldn't have even said that he'd looked very pale before, but the fact that the color was there now made its absence before seem more obvious in retrospect. She suspected that she only noticed because she had spent so much time staring at him and picturing him in her mind.

She found herself reaching out to touch his cheek. Just the slightest, soft caress, really, with the backs of her fingers along the new pinkness there. She'd almost forgotten about the heightened sense of touch they seemed to share, since...that night. She was quickly reminded.

He didn't pull away; in fact, he seemed afraid to move, but closed his eyes and drew in a slow, soft hiss of breath as she touched him. It gave her chills. "Does it hurt?" He looked at her oddly, and she realized that he was thinking of her touch in general. "The sunburn," she clarified, dropping her hand into her lap.

"Not really. It's not that noticeable, is it?"

"No, not at all. I think I only see it really because I...know you so well." Then another strange thought popped into her head. "Can you see yourself? In a mirror, I mean."

That made him smile. He always seemed amused by her spontaneous and innocent questioning. "What do you think?"

She pondered a moment. "Well," she said as she made so bold as to brush her hand along his cheek again, "you're always clean-shaven." She knitted her eyebrows for a moment as she took back her hand. "But maybe that doesn't change anymore. Then again, judging by the way that Sindy applies her makeup..."

That brought forth some laughter from him. It made her smile to see him laugh. He often seemed so sad. "No, we can't see our reflections. And it took me a long time and a lot of bloodshed to learn how to shave this way, I can assure you."

She gazed at him thoughtfully. She had a hard time believing he would ever want to hurt her. She had never had such a sweet and gentle connection with a man she was so attracted to before. Of course, she had never been quite this attracted to anyone else, but the time they shared always seemed so unique. He didn't fit the categories reserved for other guys.

Other guys usually fell into one of two categories. Either they were nothing special to her, like Todd. He was nice, she liked him, but he just didn't do anything for her. There was no spark. Or, the guys she did feel attracted to, also made her feel nervous and uncomfortable. Inevitably she would say and do things that seemed foolish and silly because she was just so infatuated with them, she couldn't be herself.

Then there was Ben. He didn't seem to fit into any category either. He also was unlike any other guy she had known. Mostly because she did feel comfortable around him and could be herself without feeling foolish, even though he was very good-looking. Yes, she would definitely consider Ben attractive, but he also seemed to argue with her incessantly, so she hadn't the chance to be nervous around him.

She had used the word infatuation when describing her feelings for Cain to Ben, but that wasn't really true anymore. This had now moved beyond infatuation. Cain was different. Cain made her feel as though she could talk to him about anything, ask him anything, and be herself without repercussions. And yet it was hard to say that she felt *comfortable* around him because she was so attracted to him that it had driven her to distraction, even before he had bitten her. Now with a heightened perception of it, she felt hard-pressed to keep her train of thought. She suddenly remembered what had sparked the question of reflection. "The sunburn...you were outside, in the daytime?"

"I got caught a bit further from home than I'd expected. It's alright, it wasn't for long and luckily the clouds held. I managed to get here none the worse for it."

"But...you were outside, in the daytime?" she repeated incredulously.

"I thought that was made clear. I know, it can be difficult to let go of closely held myths. You have to realize, the rules you've seen in the movies were created for dramatic tension, not authenticity. Only direct sunlight would truly hurt me. Going outside in the day is not a favored pastime, but it can be done. Though I must admit, I've not met many brave enough to test the boundaries. I guess I've grown a bit cocky in my old age."

She stared at him in disbelief. "What were you doing outside?"

"Nothing I'd a right to be. A bit of espionage for the three of you, actually. Although I suppose it's for naught. The sun's nearly down already."

"What are you talking about?"

"Last night, well, this morning actually, I followed them; Sindy and her lot. They'd no idea I was there. Of that, I'm sure. I thought if I could determine their place of rest, Benjamin might appreciate the information."

She sorted that out in her mind. "Sindy and the others, you followed them to where they live? I don't understand why. Ben, Alyson, and I couldn't hope to fight them, even with your help. There's too many of them and they're far too strong."

"We might take them if we were prepared, but that's not what I meant. You're forgetting, you have a great advantage at your disposal. Sunlight. It's the greatest weapon there is against our kind. If you knew where they slept, you might find a way to bring it down upon them."

As that sank in, she began to feel very uncomfortable with the idea. "That sounds awful."

"It is awful. So is what they'd do to you if they'd the chance. I can't expect you to be thankful that I...marked you, but you should be grateful for its benefits. To think of you in their hands..." He shook his head and looked away from her.

"So, you were thinking that Ben should approach them in the day? Just...get rid of them all?"

"Well, I must admit that I hadn't properly thought that through. Self-defense, I am usually pretty good at, tactical warfare, I am not. Contrary to my undead nature, I haven't much desire or stomach for harming others. Your arrival now makes me realize that Sindy would be fully aware of Ben's approach before he got within twenty feet of her. He couldn't sneak up on her. I don't think her senses have quite the range of mine, but it would be enough to warn her well. I suppose that's what they're for."

"I could do it," she offered.

"**No**," he replied forcefully.

"Allie and I they wouldn't feel us coming. Allie's mark from Sindy is gone."

"Yours from me is highly evident, my dear, not just to me, but to all vampires. That's why I gave it to you. I didn't give you nearly as much as Sindy passed into Ben, so it won't last as long, but it's quite clear at the moment."

Felicity felt her cheeks heating again as he spoke of it. The topic must seem an everyday thing to him, but to her, it was illicit and risqué. She tried not to be affected by memories of the act and pressed on. "Alyson, then. She could do it," she suggested.

"If she didn't get them all, she'd be marked for death."

"I wonder if she'll live much longer anyway." She hadn't really meant to say that; she had thought out loud, without meaning to. She looked up to find Cain staring at her. "Cain, do you know Mattie?"

He seemed to find this a strange turn for the conversation. "Ben's friend?" She nodded. He gave a slight smile. "Yes, quite well, actually. I came across him soon after he was turned. I taught him a few things and helped him adjust. I like him. He's got commendable strength of will, for one so young. He reminds me of my own stubborn abstinence, actually."

"He doesn't drink people's blood?"

"No. Well, not without...consent." He had been looking into her eyes as he said it. She wondered if he was trying to imply something. She hoped not; that was a frightening prospect that she wasn't ready to deal with at the moment. He must have noted her reaction. "Don't be so surprised. It's not as uncommon as you might think."

"I'm not, really." She looked away, embarrassed. "In fact, I kind of knew." She looked into his eyes once again. "Alyson is worried for him."

This was clearly something Cain had not expected to hear. "Alyson? That girl does constantly astonish me. I never know what to expect from her. I must admit, it's usually rather annoying, but this is odd news. Does she see him often?"

"He never mentioned her?"

"I haven't seen him in months, and it wasn't here. Besides, that's information one does not traditionally share. If she wore his mark, I would know. If she does not, she is fair game for another. To mention her as favored would merely put her at risk. Not from me, of course, but that is usually the way of things."

"He told her he would return soon. She's afraid that he may run into Arif, or Sindy, and be waylaid, I suppose."

"Well, I haven't seen him, but I will keep watch for his arrival. He would make a welcome ally right now. Although I wouldn't want to have to announce it to Ben."

"Allie told him. It wasn't pretty." She looked at him wonderingly. "Can I ask you a question?"

"You can ask me anything, and you often do. It's a little off-putting, I must say, but I've come to enjoy it. Ask away," he answered with a mischievous grin.

She smiled but felt in a much more serious mood than she had been. Something had occurred to her that wouldn't leave her head. "Ben said something, which I must admit, frightened me more than a little." Cain's smile quickly turned to concern. "I know he's wrong, Allie even said so, but I can't stop thinking about it."

"What is it?"

"When you became a vampire, did it change you? Other than physically, I mean. The way you are now, the man you are now, is this who you were? Is this what you were like in life?"

He became very still, gazing into her eyes. "Everyone changes." He looked away, uncomfortably. "It was a traumatic experience, to say the least. And, more than three hundred years certainly can't pass without leaving their mark, but I don't believe that's what you're asking.

The one who made me was thorough at least, for that I can be thankful. When it's rushed or done poorly, well, you've seen the sad results of such attempts. I've got all the memories of my life past, whether I want them or not. I wasn't aware of any change in that respect. It's not as though another being has completely taken over my body, but I suppose I have changed. For the worse and for the better, too, if you can believe it.

I can only tell you this, I don't try to be the man that I was. I didn't much like myself back then, but I don't really think I've lost anything of who I was. There's just been something else added to me. It can be difficult and frightening at times, but I much prefer the being I am now to the man I was then.

Have you ever seen the cartoons, where someone's got a devil perched upon one shoulder and an angel on the other? I feel as though I walk around with them every moment. The vampire whispers dreadful things in my ear and urges my body to unspeakable longings. Then the new man I long to be, on the other side, whispers back, tales of good deeds done and battles yet to fight.

I sometimes wish to close my eyes forever and end it all, just so I might finally have some peace. It would be nice to feel alone in my head for a change. I don't mean to frighten you, but to answer your question. I don't really know. Does it matter? *This* is the man I am now. For what it's worth, I rather hope he meets your approval."

She was gazing into his eyes and, without realizing, had leaned a bit forward into him as he spoke, intent upon his every word. She felt anguished over the things he must have endured in his life. He seemed such a sweet and gentle soul, undeserving of such trials.

Of course, who was she to say? She knew nothing of his true past. He seemed to think he deserved what had happened to him. Was he really so despicable in life that he preferred this undead existence? Whatever sort of man he had been in the past, the way in which he conducted his life now spoke volumes, considering how difficult it must be.

Now, as he completed his response to her question, she was suddenly brought back to the present and was more than lightly aware of his proximity. She wanted nothing more than to tilt her face to his for a kiss, long-awaited and frequently imagined. A shiver of anticipation went through her as she remembered the last time she'd sampled his lips, and that was before this new heightened sense of touch they seemed to share.

She fought back the urge and very deliberately brought herself to sit fully upright again. He had obviously been very aware of the moment, but let her come to her own decision, watching silently. She felt she should clarify just what he should expect from her. Saying it out loud might convince her own body to follow her mind's intentions as well.

"I don't want to go away, but that doesn't mean that I'm going to... I don't know what I want, not yet. This all needs to be taken care of, Sindy, Arif, and the others. I need to know that's under control and put it all behind us. Then I can think about...other things. Right now, I just... I don't know what I want, except that I want to stay. Is it safe for me to stay?"

He seemed to consider her question for a long time. Then again, maybe he was only memorizing her face; she couldn't tell. He finally spoke in a quiet, confident voice. "I'll make it so."

They stared at each other in silence. This new, magical awareness of his body was nearly overpowering. It seemed almost masochistic to force herself to sit so close to him without allowing him to touch her. She knew it would be beyond her wildest imaginings if she surrendered herself to it. She stood and walked away from him a pace, forcing herself to hold firm to her convictions.

"I should go check on Ben and Allie. When I left, things were kind of explosive. If I leave them alone for too long, they might kill each other." She looked back to smile at him. The expression on his face seemed almost to be bewildered admiration. She imagined that he was surprised to see how strongly in control of herself she was and her devotion to her friends.

It had been a very difficult thing not to succumb to the moment. So much harder than she had expected, that she questioned her judgment in letting herself follow him down here. She had grossly underestimated the temptation. She was afraid that, if he had been so inclined, he could easily have persuaded her to surrender herself to him. In fact, she was almost certain that he could have, but he had not. He had let her be the one to choose. She would not forget that.

He seemed to admire her all the more for her decision, but did look quite forlorn that she was leaving. "Did you want to come?" she asked. She looked around for a window to see if the sun had gone down yet, but realized that, of course, they were all covered. "I could wait."

Cain smiled. "The sun has set, but no. As much as it pains me to deny myself your company, I don't think that I'm someone Ben would like to see right now."

Cain had never spoken openly of how he felt about her before today. Of course, it was implied, and she'd known that he was attracted to her, but she couldn't remember him ever really saying it, until today. She was flattered to have the full attention of someone who could surely choose any girl he'd like. She tried very hard not to dwell on it; she had other concerns right now.

He continued, "Besides, I think I'll be needing to do some damage control of my own. Discuss my proposition with Ben and Alyson if you'd like. The others may change their location, but what was done once can be done again. Will you be in your room later, if I've any news?"

"I'm not sure. I'm going to stop over at Allie's first. I don't know how long I'll stay. Here, I'll give you her number." She fished around in her purse for a paper and pen to copy the information for him. She found them and quickly did so, although as she wrote, she found it hard to picture him doing something as mundane as calling her on the telephone. She didn't even think it likely that he *had* a phone, but he could call from Tommy's or somewhere.

He stood so close, watching over her shoulder as she wrote. She felt she had to leave...now. She hadn't realized how hard it would be to be alone in his company for any length of time. It was like a constant struggle not to give herself to him. It seemed to be getting stronger the longer she stayed. Again, she wondered what he felt and how he hid it so well.

He followed her as she climbed the stairs and opened the door for her. She turned to say goodbye, but he just looked at her quizzically. "You're not walking all the way back alone."

She looked out the door, up at the sky. Technically, the sun had set, but the sky still glowed with shades of pink and orange, more than bright enough to light her way. She nodded toward the receding colors of the brilliant sunset. "That doesn't bother you?"

"It's a bit uncomfortable, but I can handle it. That's why I brought up this." He lifted his arm to show that he'd draped a black leather jacket across it. She noticed he'd brought up his denim as well. "I saw that you didn't bring a jacket, so I took the liberty."

He handed her the denim. She smiled at him and put it on. It was a little big, but she felt inexplicably reassured by it. It smelled lightly of his aftershave. "Thanks. It's not all that cold."

"You'll need it if we take the bike. I'd rather walk, but I suppose that would just be a selfish ploy to stretch out our time together. I guess it's no big secret at this point that I do cherish time with you. I hope you enjoy it as well. Unfortunately, it's usually spent chasing, fighting, and running from other vampires, but I can't think of anyone else I'd rather do it with.

Perhaps one night we can share a quiet evening of pleasant thoughts. However, tonight you need to see to your friends, and I need to check on things as well. As you said, the quicker we get all of this under control and behind us, the better."

He pulled a pair of dark sunglasses from his pocket, put them on, and outstretched his hand for her to step out onto the porch. She made her way down the steps to the motorcycle and noticed a new helmet perched on the seat. She turned to him. "Been shopping?"

"I figured your life's been in enough danger lately. Why take a stupid chance?"

Felicity smiled and put it on as Cain got on the bike. She hopped up behind him and got herself settled, with her hands holding him around the waist. It felt good to be touching him, even through the leather. She wondered just how much of it was her own passion and how much was this strange connection they now shared.

He took off down the road. She was enjoying the ride, even reveling in the little thrill it gave her to be pressed up against him. She wondered if it affected him at all. The feeling from the mark certainly went both ways; he'd indicated as much, but did it really excite him to be close to her? She began to realize that although she did trust him, it might be unfair and maybe unwise to tempt him too much by being alone with him for too long, or too often. She could guess the things that the imagined vampire perched on his shoulder would be whispering, and she'd do better not to press her luck.

He began to slow as they entered town, and she realized that he probably didn't know where Alyson lived. As they reached the corner after Tommy's, she gave his left leg a little squeeze with her own, as though she were riding a horse, while also nudging him a bit with her left arm. He understood her perfectly and made the turn without comment. In this way, she directed him until they reached Allie's. Her car was not there.

Felicity got off the bike and removed the helmet. Cain took it from her and strapped it to the bar on the back of the seat. She watched him and then moved closer to say goodbye. She was sorely tempted again to kiss him, but that was something she was better off not starting now. It would be sending mixed signals.

Besides, the last place she wanted to allow herself to kiss him was in Allie's driveway with Ben probably looking out the window. She settled for lightly resting her hand on top of his, on the handlebar of the bike. She looked into his eyes as a little thrill raced through her at the contact. He looked back into hers for a long time. Finally, she dropped her hand. "Maybe you should wait until I see if anyone's here. Allie's car isn't back."

"Ben's inside," Cain assured her.

"How do you... Oh," she amended as she realized he could see Ben's new mark.

"I don't think I'll see you later, but I'll find you tomorrow night. Or, if you'd like to come again, sooner..."

She smiled and gave a little non-committal shrug. "Goodnight. Oh…" She began to take off the jacket to give it back.

"Keep it for now. You can give it back tomorrow." With that, he walked the bike back down the driveway, revved the motor, and rode off down the road. She quickly found herself alone in the cool night. The breeze had picked up, and the clouds were racing across the sky as it turned shades of purple and dark blue with the nightfall.

She started up the front walk, contemplating her receding sense of him. Her body practically ached to feel him moving away. And he hadn't given her a full measure of the venom? Perhaps it had a more potent effect on her because she desired him anyway. She didn't know, but it was quite distracting. Poor Ben. She strongly hoped that Sindy would not come anywhere near him tonight.

Chapter 8 – Motives

Cain

An empty field
10:00, Sunday night

Cain sat in the field next to the cemetery, playing with a blade of grass in his hand. He'd been sitting here for some time, unconcealed, waiting. He wasn't sure what else to do. He wanted to speak with Sindy, but another outburst in a public place full of onlookers did not appeal. He didn't want to wander around looking for her. His intentions would surely be misread. He simply wanted to talk, for now.

He had begun to feel that his reaction early this morning was a bit overly dramatic. Would he really have let Ben kill them? He wasn't sure. Undoubtedly, it had all seemed very harsh and tense at the time, but now that it was over, he did see that no serious damage had been done. Ben may not agree, but at least he was alive.

Cain's true motive had been to try to make sure that he did not lose Felicity. She was still receptive to him, though much more poised and in control of herself than he might have thought she'd be. At least he knew she wouldn't entirely shun him. That accomplished, he didn't find himself as furious with Sindy as he probably should have been.

Felicity did still care for him, or she wouldn't have come to see him. Sindy's words may have spooked her a little, but she hadn't completely recoiled from him. He was also sure his bite had produced a potent effect in her; yet she did not let herself bend to its will. That hadn't really been his purpose in biting her, but he was a little surprised. It made her all the more alluring. Much more enticing than if she openly craved his attentions. He had come to respect her strength of will.

It was always hard to tell how a person would react to being bitten. Of course, it wasn't something ever openly studied or recorded. A certain amount of information was passed to a new vampire from their sire, but the venom was almost lost knowledge. Frankly, he was amazed that Sindy knew so much about it. It certainly wasn't something they had ever discussed. That was information Cain usually withheld when possible. Why tempt them?

Most killed when they drank. If their victims felt its effect, it made drinking that much easier, but it would hardly be noticed by the predator. As modern times made killing much more difficult to accomplish without notice, more and more vampires were learning to leave their victims still clinging to life.

The mark that came with this was now common knowledge, but as far as Cain knew, mostly it served as a warning to a vampire, to identify one who might give them trouble in knowing their true nature. Or it led a vampire back to a person that they might want to revisit or turn.

It also helped to mark territory. It wouldn't do to have too many hunting the same grounds. The experience itself, of being bitten, was not something many vampires bothered to inquire about of their victims. They had only their own experience to remember.

Cain did know that his venom seemed to grow more potent as he aged. It was difficult to gauge because every person's experience varied. And of course, his experiences with humans were few and far between. But each time, he noticed that their reactions seemed to become more and more pronounced.

Felicity's was the strongest yet. He had made sure to let the venom enter her system before drinking any of her blood. Once he was sure that his venom was within her, she was marked. He hadn't really needed to drink from her at all, but that was just asking for too much self-control. Even he couldn't expect that much of himself, but he had only taken the slightest taste.

He had hardly even fed from her, and yet her reaction had seemed drastically increased, compared to the last person he'd infected. Perhaps she was more vulnerable to it for some reason, but he didn't really think so. It was him; his body's abilities were increasing with age. She had clung to him in a way that he had found incredibly arousing, and he'd had to summon considerable will to force himself from her. He pushed the memory away before it led to things that he should not even imagine right now.

Thinking of the venom caused him again to wonder what Ben's reaction had been like. Sindy was newborn compared to Cain, and there was no telling how such things would vary from vampire to vampire, but she had taken her time and been sure to infect him well with her evil serum. Such a dose would certainly have some effect. He was certain that Sindy hoped so. Ben should be well attuned to her.

Felicity was definitely well attuned to him, as he was to her. Admittedly, since the time of the bite itself, he had begun to wonder about its effects. She hid it remarkably well, but today assured him that a heightened desire was in fact there; she simply kept her feelings in check.

That she remained able to hold herself aloof from him still was almost amazing to him. The beast in the back of his mind coaxed him to realize that this was easily remedied. A fuller sampling would certainly bring her to him, but that was not his desire, not truly. He wanted her to be sure, but not like that. What would be the point? He could have done that a month ago if her physical acceptance had been his only aspiration.

He'd been sitting out here alone in the field for some time, pondering these things. Then his mind turned back to Sindy. As angry as she usually made him and as hard as she might try to provoke a reaction, or solicit sexual favors from him, what he found himself feeling for her more and more was pity. She would be enraged if she ever thought so, but he had begun to see her as someone who had been so hurt, rejected, unloved, and abused that she knew of no other way to gain favor, or at least some attention from others, than the things that she did.

Her actions last night spoke to him not of petty revenge and backlash towards him, although they were certainly so motivated. What it had really seemed to him was a cry for help. A plea for attention and acceptance. All of her talk about proving herself worthy for him, from a girl with her tenacity of spirit? She was infuriated that she could not gain worth in his eyes; he was sure of it.

Of course, the easiest way for her to meet his approval would be to follow his example, as far as feeding habits were concerned, but she had far too rebellious a nature to give in so easily to his demands. She insisted on having people believe that everything she did was on her own terms. Perhaps she even felt the need to prove that to herself.

The wiles she was most accustomed to using on men had not prevailed with him. She was very used to being valued for her body. He had not accepted her advances. He had turned her away, and she didn't know how to bring him back. It tormented her, probably for the principal, more than actually wanting him. She wanted to be in control. Even if she drove him to kill her, at least it would be by her actions and decree.

She approached. Marcus was with her. Wonderful. A bodyguard, he supposed. At least she brought no one else. He didn't bother to get up. He was lying back on his elbows, looking up at the stars. Let her see that he had no fear of her; it would probably drive her mad.

She stopped about twenty feet away and smiled at his casual pose. She then turned and placed a firm hand on Marcus's chest, speaking to him quietly. 'Sit. Stay. Good boy,' Cain assumed. Marcus folded his arms and stood, looking sullen and cross. Cain had the childish urge to stick his tongue out at the man. Of course, he didn't.

Finally, Sindy sauntered toward him supremely unconcerned, not to be outdone by his lack of alarm. He eyed her for a moment and then asked with quiet sincerity, "Do you want to die?"

This rather caught her off guard. She laughed as she dropped herself to the ground to sit next to him in the tall grass. Not too close, he noticed. "Do you? Here you are, all alone, without your precious psychic shield, just waiting for me. I've got enough manpower now, I'm sure I could take you down. Hell, Marcus, there could probably do it alone."

Cain smiled. "I highly doubt it. I could run circles around that gorilla."

"Is that a fact? Then why didn't you finish him off last time? Don't try to tell me that the stake you left sticking out of him was supposed to be some kind of warning, because to me, it looked more like bad aim."

He neatly sidestepped the question. "You don't want to kill me."

"I don't?"

"Oh, heaven's no! You're far too fond of me. You seek my approval. You don't want my death; you want my respect. Which you did not earn last night, by the way. All that accomplished was to more firmly cement Ben's hatred of you. Probably not wise. I know that you think humans are easily manipulated, but don't push Benjamin and his friends too far, or it will mean your death."

She laughed. "Oh, please! What's Ben gonna do?"

"There is a Christian speaker named Beth Moore who once said that while 'a woman scorned is surely a force to be reckoned with, a man humiliated may yet be far worse. ' You don't think he's plotting your demise even as we speak?"

"Even as we speak, I think Ben's probably hiding under the covers, having himself a good wet dream."

She seemed to love trying to shock him; he found it terribly annoying. "Must you always be so crass?"

"What's the matter? Do I offend your prude old English sensibilities?"

He rolled his eyes and pressed on. "The point is, your little performance only shows how sorely you long for my attention. You wouldn't want to kill me, then you'd have no one left to try and impress. I've the feeling Arif is not at all interested. Besides, 'docile harem girl' doesn't strike me as your style."

"All submissive and obedient? Hardly! But you and Arif aren't the only fish in the sea."

"Have you shopped around? A decent vampire is hard to find. We're a rare breed."

"Conceited much? Anyway, 'decent vampire', isn't that a contradiction in terms?" She shook her head and looked up at the sky for a moment. "As flawed as your logic may be, I could still turn it around and say the same of you. You don't want to kill me, or I would have been dead a long time ago. You think you can tame me. I'm like a wild horse that you're just itchin' to break. You want to transform me into something more suitable for your arm. Like that stupid play they made us see in school...My Fair Lady."

"Ah, Pygmalion. Fancy yourself Eliza Doolittle, do you?" He laughed. "Is that what you think? Well, I'll let you in on a little secret." He paused. Like all girls, she loved secrets and eagerly hovered close to hear. He wouldn't disappoint her.

He looked into her eyes and spoke slowly and sincerely, with careful attention to each word. "You have the potential to become a truly splendid creature." He let that soak in for a moment. She wasn't sure how to accept it, whether or not he was teasing her, but she was obviously pleased. "But if you haven't the desire, then I haven't the patience. I am old, and I haven't the forbearance to wait around while you play childish games. And now you've made me go and sound like Arif, which I find most disturbing," he finished with a shake of his head.

"Maybe I've decided that you aren't worth changing for."

"I never claimed to be. And while I do allow myself a selfish motive now and again, I hadn't really been trying to get you to change for me."

"Then why do you try so hard?" she asked.

"For you." She gave him a sarcastic smirk. "For your own peace of mind and well-being, among other purposes."

"Here we go. What purposes would those be? For God? Are you trying to save my soul? 'Cause you're a little late. We're vampires, honey, and no amount of good deeds now will let you into those pearly gates! You think you're on some kind of holy mission? You're a holy joke! You are like a walking insult to God! If there even is a God and he's looking down on you, I'm thinkin' he's got to be pissed!"

"'Do not be deceived: God cannot be mocked. A man reaps what he sows. The one who sows to please his sinful nature, from that nature will reap destruction; the one who sows to please the Spirit, from the Spirit will reap eternal life.' That's Galatians 6:7 and 8. Sindy, please, I've argued these points hundreds of times with hundreds of others, far more versed in the gospel than you."

She rolled her eyes at him and shook her head. "You gonna try and tell me you don't ever please that sinful nature of yours?" He began to protest, but she wouldn't let him. "I know, I know. So you don't live off human blood. Give the man a gold star. I'm talking about Felicity and whatever other poor girls you've ruined along the way. You gonna tell me it isn't so?"

"I never claimed to be entirely righteous. We are sinners all. The most we can do is make every effort to do what is right each new day. Anyway, who are you to say that I've ruined anyone? You don't know anything of my life, and I've done nothing truly harmful to Felicity."

"Right. And you're what...in suspended animation? Where's it going? Nowhere? Give me a break! There will be a point where you cross the line.

All of this spiritual crap is not really my arena, but physical expression? Now that's something I can tell you about. I've been watching you two; I read the body language. I've gotta tell ya, I'm thinkin' there's not a whole lot goin' on. She likes you, and we both know you're hot for her. You've got the chemistry. In fact, the sexual tension between you guys is pretty thick, and isn't that fun? But there are definitely some major boundaries there. So, what's the holdup, Cain? You wanna take your time, make it all sweet and meaningful? 'Cause anyone you're gonna waste that much effort on has gotta be more than a passing fling.

You're invested in her. When things reach the limit, where else are you gonna go? You wanna tell me you're not gonna take the next step? You're just gonna walk away? 'Have a nice life.' I don't think so.

If I pushed you too far and you lost your beloved self-control and killed me, well, that's something that you could probably consider yourself beyond reproach for. I'm not innocent or pure in any sense of the word. Sending my soul to Hell would probably earn 'ya extra credit, but Felicity? You're gonna take her young life and condemn her innocent soul? Isn't that a little risky to your precious theology?"

He was shaking his head and dismissing her words before she even finished speaking. "There is no way for us to know the status or condition of one's soul. The best we can do is to conduct ourselves as one would expect a heaven-bound soul to act.

I never said that I would change Felicity to become one of us, but even if I did, if it were by her own choice and she were to live as I do, without taking human life, then who are you to say that it's wrong? There are those who see our state as being in the possession of amazing gifts. If these gifts are used for good, then are we not good as well? Everything and everyone has a purpose, and I will not believe that mine is to be evil."

"So that's the plan? Rationalize a way for you to get just what you want? If that's the plan, then you really don't need me, do you? Why bother with me at all? I've got to admit that I do spend a good part of my time trying to think of ways to put you through hell! Why don't you just call it a bad job and leave me alone already? Aren't you getting tired of fighting for a lost cause?"

"'Let us not become weary in doing good, for at the proper time we will reap a harvest if we do not give up.' That's also Galatians 6:9."

"Don't you get it? It does not apply! We're already damned! It's too late!"

"It's never too late."

"Really? When's the last time you touched a cross? Face it, Cain, we are removed from humans and all of their stupid beliefs! That stuff can't help us now. We're outcasts, and without each other, we're alone. Other vampires are all we have, and you know what? You're right, I've been around, and most of them are monsters, but guess what, so are we. We're made to be monsters. Perfect predatory killers. Why fight it?"

"Why not? When is the last time you did something because someone told you to? You think you have to become a killer just because that's what your sire led you to believe? You know already that it's not true.

You've fed without killing. You've the strength of will to live in peace with those around you, if not the desire. I know that you're strong enough. To kill and live off of others is certainly easier and usually more appealing than to have to make it on your own. To live in a responsible and civil manner is sometimes fraught with difficulty, but when isn't sin easy or appealing?

Does it really make you so happy to hurt others, or is the satisfaction it gives you fleeting and petty? Is it gratifying to surround yourself with false friends and lovers, so that you can feel secure and accepted, or is it empty and lacking? Doesn't it leave you wanting more? That's why you're never satisfied.

You could surround yourself with hundreds, but if you can't see them as equals... If you can't know that they accept you for who you are, instead of what you may do for them... If you can't deny that they cling to you in fear, whether it's fear of you, or fear of being without you...you might as well be all alone. And if you're going to be all alone, you'd better be able to live with yourself."

Sindy sat and watched him with quiet malice. She was difficult to read. She seemed very capable of suddenly shifting either way. Would she accede to his point, finally break down, and give in to the hurt and the sorrow that had surely been holding her prisoner? Ask him to help her start anew? Or would she once again hide behind her rage and build yet another mental wall between them, to keep him out? To keep herself from having to see her own insecurities.

She surprised him by choosing a path level and mature, somewhat down the middle. She was hurt and angered by the things he'd said, because she surely knew them to be true. She did not try to deny them, but she would not set aside her pride or let him in any way view her as weak. She did have the instincts of a true predator. He was surprised to see that after some thoughtful consideration, her mood seemed compromising.

"You're pretty observant. I'm observant too. I've seen the way you live, and I've gotta tell 'ya, the way you dominate the vampire in you is very impressive. I know it's not easy, especially when you've just had such a sweet reminder from Felicity of how good it can be. So, I admire your self-control.

I still think it's pointless. Why deny yourself something that you were meant to, made to have? But that's your choice, and anything that you feel that strongly about is worth taking notice of. You are older than me, so maybe you've got more experience than me, but when it comes to strength of will, you are not stronger than me. So, I'm gonna stick to what I said. I'm gonna go without for a while, just because I want you to know that I can.

In the meantime, I still think that in playing with Felicity, you are playing with fire. And I'm gonna stand back and watch you get burned. You're not a saint! You aren't meant to be, and you can't expect to resist such appetizing fare. She wants you, and I know you won't be able to hold out forever.

Maybe you could even make her happy for a while, but guess what? She's got a life! Unlike you, who have nothing else to exist for from night to night, she's got friends and family. She's going to college, so she must aspire to something in her future. Think she'll want a real live hubby, too? A couple of snot-nosed kids... Well, I guess you could always adopt!" she said with a cruel laugh. "You gonna buy her a house with a white picket fence? Face it, Cain, you are from two different walks of life, and you just don't mesh. She can't ever really be anything more to you than a plaything or a meal, unless you kill her."

He wouldn't respond. Her words forced him to look into dark truths that he usually shied from. He wouldn't go there now. It was the first time he had ever felt he had made any sort of progress with Sindy, disregarding the parts designed to hurt him. He had to admit that she was uncomfortably close to the mark, but he would deal with his own demons later.

She stood and looked down at him for a moment, then reached a hand down to help him up. It seemed such a strange gesture coming from her, and an uncomfortable one, since it immediately reminded him of his first night in the gym with Felicity. She had reached out to him in the same way, unafraid and wanting nothing more than to connect with him somehow. A simple and sincere gesture. Coming from Sindy, however, he eyed it with much more trepidation. He felt like Charlie Brown, wondering whether or not Lucy would pull the football away. Not that he had anything to lose. He accepted her hand, and she gently pulled him to his feet with a smile.

"Speaking of playful meals, I think I'll go and pay Ben a little visit. Unless you had something more appealing in mind? I've got a short attention span, and I'm done talkin'. I'm in the mood for something a little more physical."

"Why don't you go home to your playthings then?"

"I sent them out hunting. Just 'cause I'm gonna suffer, doesn't mean they should. It wouldn't be fair. Don't worry, I left Chris and Luke in charge. I know you don't approve of my boys, but they are pretty capable, as long as you keep it simple. They know the rules; nobody dies. And Marcus...well, I have to admit, he's just not turning out to be as much fun as I thought he'd be. He's useful, sure, but between you and me," she whispered to him conspiratorially, with a quick glance over to her muscle man. "The man's got no staying power." She smiled and shook her head.

She moved in even closer to him, and her voice took on the seductive tone he had grown to know so well from her. "But you must be feeling awfully frustrated night after night." She openly ran her eyes over his body, lingering here and there. "I could help you out with that; it wouldn't have to mean a thing." He just looked at her with knitted brows. Any kind of satisfaction from their talk, or budding camaraderie he might have felt for her, was immediately displaced by her words. Why could she never just let things be?

She assessed his mood and continued. "No, huh? Well, lucky Ben. You don't mind, do you? I wouldn't want you to be jealous."

"I thought you were going to stay away from him now. Wasn't that part of your inane agreement? You should know that I have promised Felicity that she and her friends will not be harmed again. I will enforce that if necessary. As you pointed out, killing you and yours would not be something I would suffer over."

"Oh, relax. I'm not gonna do anything, unless he begs me to, I mean. You wouldn't expect me to actually turn him away, would you? But if you want to get technical, I get what you get, remember? An eye for an eye. Don't tell me you haven't seen her.

Besides, how can you make me miss out on such fun? I've been waiting for Ben to appreciate me for years. He may never admit it, but damn if I'm not gonna make that boy want me!" Cain just rolled his eyes and shook his head. "You know he's safe inside some house somewhere that I can't enter into anyway. So what if I want to sit outside the window? Is that against any of your grand edicts? At least you'll know where I am, and you should be happy that I'm not out wreaking havoc and destruction. Hell, what am I asking you for anyway? I can do what I want. I'm out of here."

She blew him a kiss and returned to Marcus, who had been waiting as a statue the entire time. Cain let her go without a word. He was heartened that she didn't really want to risk his anger anymore. In fact, the entire evening she had conducted herself with a considerable amount of maturity and better thought-out arguments than he had ever expected. Perhaps there was hope for her yet.

At the moment, Cain's interest was hopelessly captured by Felicity. An interest that, however unwise, he knew he would find himself unable to ignore. Sindy's words cruelly repeated themselves in his head. She can't ever really be anything more to you than a plaything or a meal, unless you kill her. That didn't have to be true…did it? He tried to believe that he was stronger than that, although in truth, he was uncertain.

Felicity had awoken stirrings in his still heart that brought him hope and joy he'd thought forgotten. He had to see her again. He could only hope he was making the right decision. He also did believe the prediction he had voiced earlier. Sindy could indeed become a truly splendid creature, with just the right amount of guidance. He wondered if she might even be worth waiting for.

~~~~~~~~~~~~~~~~~~~~~~~~~~~~~~~~

To Be Continued
In

ALMOST HUMAN

~ The First Series ~

PERSISTENT PERSUASION

(Lost Reflections – Part 1)

~~~~~~~~~~~~~~~~~~~~~~~~~~~~~~~~

If you enjoyed this book, please take a moment to leave a review online,
on your favorite book review website!

You can learn more about the characters, read cast interviews, and get
updates on upcoming book releases for this series on the author's
website at www.MelanieNowak.com